# The Unadoptables

## No One Hears Their Cries

PJ Dischino

Editor: Cynthia Krejcsi

ckrejcsi@yahoo.com


Cover photograph:

Flickr image Reese Is Sad by Donnie Ray Jones

https://creativecommons.org/licenses/by-sa/4.0/legalcode

ISBN-10: 0692941169
ISBN-13: 978-0692941164

# DEDICATION

To all those in my life who have contributed to my eighty plus years of experiences, especially the children. A special thanks to my editor, Cynthia Krejcsi, who is always there to rescue me.

# CONTENTS

**MARIE**

**NICHOLAS**

**MARIE**

**NICHOLAS**

**MARIE**

**NICHOLAS**

**LILY, MARIE, NICHOLAS**

PJ Dischino

LILY

# Chapter 1

Four-year-old Lily sat on the gray-pitted concrete steps picking at a small hole on her right sneaker. Bright yellow in a previous life, the shoes were now reduced to a washed-out, hand-me-down hue. The footwear matched the outfit she had picked that morning from her brown cardboard suitcase labeled "Lily." The long-sleeved shirt had a rainbow arched across the front, but the depth of its colors was almost imperceptible now.

A van with the name "Drayton House" emblazoned on its front door, also faded with years of use, drove up the narrow driveway close to the steps where Lily waited. As the driver, Ben, opened the passenger door, he surveyed the neglected yard so typical of the drop-off placements where shelter children found themselves spending the night. It saddened Ben that this was the best society could do for its most vulnerable members.

"Hi Lily! Hop in," Ben called out.

The first cheery note of the day reached Lily's ears, and a slight smile crinkled her usually solemn face.

"How did it go last night, Pretty Flower?"

"Bad, Ben. They were mean to me. I was cold when I went to bed. There was a blanket with holes and it was thin. Two girls called me stupid and ugly. They said it again at breakfast."

"Didn't the parents say anything?"

"Yes, but they didn't really care. I was so scared. I didn't know where the bathroom was at night. It was dark. I started to cry. The lady came in and gave me a little flashlight. She kept shushing me. And nobody said goodbye to me this morning. They were mean."

"Well, you know you are not ugly or stupid. You are as beautiful as a flower. You learned English and taught yourself how to read. I call that very smart."

Ben, as the jack-of-all-trades at Drayton House, dealt with the institution's various requirements. A white-haired, tall and slender widower in his late sixties, he lived alone in a small brick cottage at the end of the shelter's property. Ben lovingly maintained his little home.

As a retired officer from the New Jersey State Police Force, Ben received an ample pension. He and his wife had led a simple but comfortable life until she died. Now that she was gone, simplicity sufficed.

Although Ben was childless, he had a built-in kindness that radiated warmth and attracted children to him. The fact that the children in the shelter were so in need of emotional warmth but received little more than basic care saddened him to no end. He tried to spread tiny rays of cheer to the shelter's residents.

It was an unwritten law that he was never to have any of the children enter his cottage. This was understandable given all the reports of child abuse broadcast over the airways. But it was ironic that Ben, who exhibited a most ethical and unblemished character, was denied visits while unsavory rumors of dark behavior passed the lips of those who worked or were placed within the shelter walls. In fact, fifteen years earlier the previous manager of Drayton had committed atrocious crimes that gave the shelter a black name.

Lily's story was the most poignant at the shelter. Children at Drayton usually spent a minimum of time there. They either went back to their homes or were placed in long-term foster homes. A few lucked out and were adopted. But Lily's case precluded long-term foster care or adoption. "Unadoptable" had been stamped boldly on all of Lily's documents. A family wishing to adopt Lily might have been able to overturn that label, but so far no one had even been interested.

When she was only two years old, Lily had been put into a wheelchair and left in a dark corner of the Newark airport. Invisible to passersby, Lily remained there for hours, until she finally got out of the chair and walked where people could see her. She spoke no

English but pointed to herself, repeating what sounded like "Lily bu yat sa."

A large crowd gathered around her. The words that Lily said passed quickly around. An elderly woman pushed her way forward. "I am Russian, and I understand her. She is saying, 'Lily's scared.'"

It was as if Lily fell from a celestial sphere. Loudspeakers filled the airport with frantic pleas for information. No one came forward. There hadn't even been a plane arriving from Russia that day, so her appearance was a real mystery.

Lily was taken to a local shelter, where she stayed for several weeks. When the search for details reached a dead end, Drayton finally became her home. Because it was possible that at some point someone might turn up to claim a relationship to Lily, she was labeled "unadoptable."

Since the majority of children at the shelter were temporary residents, they received almost no quality time with staff members. Financial restraints often precluded giving emotional, lost children a fair share of attention or education. Something as simple as a temporary illness was an annoyance to the management. A child who appeared to be exploding with germs had to spend the night at the shelter instead of being sent out to stay with a family. Shelters did not take kindly to sick children because it meant they had to add personnel to their skeleton night crew.

Employees at the shelter were not necessarily mean-spirited, but they were only working at the shelter as a means of employment. Most were living on the edge of financial disaster and emotional vulnerability themselves, so they didn't have much energy left to expend on someone else's children.

Since she was so young, Lily did not have the savvy to shake off insults. Words like *ugly, stupid,* and *dirty* swirled in her head. Often she tried to settle on what these words meant for her. Was she ugly? What do ugly people look like? Lily didn't think she was stupid. She had taught herself to read. No one else her age or even older kids had this skill. Her faded yellow shirt that had been worn by so many children before her had small stains permanently set into the fabric. To her, THAT was ugly.

"Could we go by the Duck Pond?" Lily asked Ben on the way back to the shelter. Her words were barely audible. She knew they were running late. Ben had picked up five other shelter children from locations on the other side of Oakland and dropped them off at Drayton. Then he made a separate trip to pick up Lily.

There was something noteworthy about Ben and Lily's relationship. They truly liked each other, which was unusual in a shelter setting.

"It's really late, but let's do it."

Sweet anticipation lifted Lily's tiny spirit.

"Thank you, Ben."

"My pleasure."

Ben always had a loaf or two of stale bread tucked in the back of the van for just such occasions. He looked into the rear-view mirror to catch the spark of change in Lily's face. Her solemn expression vanished, replaced by a dimpled smile indicating her pleasure. Ben's emotions swirled between delight and despair over the simplicity of his gift and the magnitude of the results.

It seemed like it took forever to get there, but soon Lily was bouncing on the banks of the pond located in a park much too far from where they were supposed to be.

"There's Greenie!" Lily shouted, pointing to a Mallard paddling as if its life depended on reaching the target, which happened to be her.

The fact that there was a bond between a duck and a child amazed Ben. There were other children tossing bread to hungry recipients, but Greenie never moved from his secluded spot across the pond until Lily appeared. When he saw her, he waddled right up to her and took the bread from the gleeful child's hands.

All too soon, it was time for Lily to leave what she loved to do and go back to a place where she found little pleasure. Time at the pond was too short while time at the shelter was forever. Her smile was soon replaced by an expression of stoic acceptance.

# Chapter 2

The dour expression on the face of Mrs. Andrews, the shelter manager, ruled out any warm reception for Ben and Lily as they came in through the back door of Drayton House.

"Jeez Ben, where the hell have you been? You were supposed to pick up the food from the Food Bank. I was going to use the flour to make fish cakes. Now it's too late."

As Mrs. Andrews finished her diatribe, she pushed Lily towards the dormitory, where the little girl's few belongings were stored. She did not ask one question about how the sleepover had gone for Lily.

"Change your clothes and brush your teeth. Didn't they do anything for you last night?"

Without even waiting for an answer, the manager rushed out to attend to what she considered more important than a brief conversation about a small child's needs. She left to oversee lunch.

The tender link between Lily and Ben was temporarily severed as Lily went to do Mrs. Andrews' bidding. But the brief time at the pond with Ben and Greenie endured, if only in her thoughts. Lily wasn't ready to let them slip away.

Lily had learned early on that complaining was a waste of time. The staff at Drayton House was not malicious. They were just mainly concerned with their own lives, avoiding problems at all costs.

The one exception was a part-time employee named Mrs. Romero, Rose to the Drayton staff. Rose had been hired to assist with the children's educational needs, which mostly meant homework assignments.

Rose was amazed at Lily's advanced competency for her age. When handed a third-grade problem-solving book, Lily answered a third of the questions at one sitting. Rose pointed this out to the manager and anyone who would listen, but the staff made little of it.

At lunch, seven unsmiling children sat at the worn wooden table used for meals. Their somberness was the result of the lack of joy a dysfunctional childhood creates. Three of the children were new. One immediately bore witness to his dislike of those around him as well as life in general. He was a tall brute of a boy in his early teens. Unpleasant recollections of him materialized from his previous stint at Drayton. Lily's stomach ached as it always did when fear set in.

When no one was looking, he had taunted Lily, stolen her paint set and coloring book, and eaten her dinner. Food was the least important thing to Lily, but the loss of her paint set and coloring book hurt deeply. When Ben had given them to her at Christmas, he warned her that someone was likely to steal them. Ben had offered to keep them at his cottage and bring them over any time she asked. But Lily loved the set so much she wanted to have it with her all the time. Then it was gone. Ben had replaced the set, but the hurt remained.

The brute had a name—Luke. And as soon as he recognized Lily, he began his strong-arm tactics with mean-spirited glee.

"What a creep you are. I'm going to make you miserable this afternoon. You and the others better do everything I tell you to do. Otherwise you'll pay. Creepy little bitch, give me your lunch," he demanded, eyeballing Lily with pure hatred.

At that moment there was no adult in the room, so there was little for Lily to do but comply. She trudged over to Luke's seat on wobbly legs. Luke grabbed the dish with one hand while with the other he pushed the terrified child, causing her to fall against the sharp edge of the table. Blood spurted from the resulting gash.

Lily's screams filled the air, and immediately two of the kitchen help raced in and tried to handle the situation. By now Lily had passed out, so they carried the little wounded creature to a nearby room and placed her down on a small couch. Then they called police security and the paramedics.

But before they arrived, Ben rushed in. He'd been outside repairing the fence protecting his vegetable garden when he heard Lily scream. Ben was sitting with her when she regained consciousness.

"Ben, that bad boy pushed me," Lily whimpered as the blood trickled down her face and covered the tiny fingers that were searching for the wound.

Suddenly Mrs. Andrews bolted out of her office. She immediately realized the potential consequences of the situation. As manager of Drayton, it was her main responsibility to provide safety for those in her care. Obviously, she had failed to do so.

Mrs. Andrews was not malevolent, but she was austere and sorely lacked any empathetic graces. But when she saw Lily covered in blood, guilt permeated her being while lighting up her soul with compassion for the first time. An innocent child had been put in jeopardy because a paramount rule of shelters had been broken: Never leave children without adult supervision. These were troubled children, often with anger issues. Mrs. Andrews knew Luke's reputation. She was ultimately responsible for this situation. Now her life as she knew it could be obliterated as a result of her neglect.

Ali, one of the staff members, caught Ben's eye and pointed to Luke, who was leaning against the wall. A waxen look had replaced his earlier expression of bravado.

Ben grabbed Luke with one hand while bending his arm back with the other. Luke's brazen attitude was reduced to that of a sniveling coward as he writhed in the old man's painful grip.

Ben snarled, "If you ever touch any child here again, I will beat you so badly you will wish you were dead. If you ever go near Lily, you WILL be dead. If you tell anyone what I have said to you, you will spend years in jail. I am an ex-cop and I have lots of friends."

With that, he dropped Luke onto a chair. By now, the bully was himself beyond fear.

# Chapter 3

Ben washed as much blood away from Lily's bruised face as he could without touching the wound on the side of her head. Matted hair caused by clotted blood made it difficult to assess the severity of the cut.

When the EMS arrived, the technician determined Lily would need stitches. There was also a concern that she might have a concussion since she had been unconscious for a brief time. Ben insisted on riding to the hospital with the EMS. Lily certainly needed an advocate. The ambulance headed for Mt. Carmel, the hospital where the attending pediatrician headed the children's section. She was a doctor for whom Ben had the highest regard, as well as a deep personal fondness.

"Marie, EMS just arrived with a Drayton child," an attractive redhead with a thick Irish brogue informed the tall brunette doctor who was attending a young patient.

"Really? in emergency?"

"I think so."

"I'm finished here, Siobhan. After I deliver this young man to his mom, I'm on my way," Dr. Eagan assured her colleague and best friend.

Dr. Marie Eagan's childhood from hell had taken place in Drayton. The label "unadoptable" was a stigma Marie still could not shake loose, even though it had no bearing on her adult life.

Marie raced down the two flights to Emergency. She saw Ben's concerned face before she reached the patient. That beloved face was a part of her own childhood, probably the *only* good part.

Wrapping her arms tightly around his shoulders, she asked, "Ben, what's going on at the shelter? Is it the same shit, with the staff still cheating children of their childhood? Why are you the only one who cares?"

"Almost the same shit, Marie. I haven't heard of any sexual abuse, but everyone is very tight lipped."

The conversation continued until they reached the gurney where the softly whimpering child lay. Ben referred to Lily's "unadoptable" status, and Dr. Eagan's expression darkened as her body stiffened. But she quickly put on a smile as she approached Lily. This poor little waif did not need to be treated by an angry doctor.

Ben took a seat nearby, close enough to give information if necessary. Next to him was a young policeman still trying to gather all the facts.

Dr. Eagan put her hands gently on Lily's shoulders, softly massaging the thin arms protruding from a bloody shirt.

"Little sweetheart Lily, what happened to you?"

As the beautiful young doctor spoke, her gentle hands investigated the gash as best she could. She asked Ben if Lily had lost consciousness at all. When Ben said "yes," Dr. Eagan made a quick decision. Not only would Lily need stitches, but an overnight stay for observation was certainly called for as well.

She asked Lily who had done this terrible thing to her.

"A bad boy pushed me and I fell."

"Oh, what a mean thing to do to such a sweet, beautiful girl."

"Everybody's mean . . . except Ben . . . and Rose."

Then looking into the doctor's eyes, the still whimpering child added, "and you."

The words penetrated Dr. Eagan's entire being. This child's emotional pain was the same burden she had carried as a child and still did as an adult.

"Well, guess what, little girl. You are going to stay with us for a while. I am going to fix your cut, and of course you are going to have to eat lots of ice cream and listen to stories. Are you ready for that?"

The whimpering stopped abruptly. This lady's musical voice soothed the scared little girl. She was just like a princess right out of the fairy tales Lily loved.

Ben came over and told her that he had known Dr. Eagan for many years. "She's the best, Pretty Flower. She'll take good care of you. I'll pick you up tomorrow or whenever you're all better."

Lily gave a small wave goodbye as an aide piloted her gurney to a little bit of heaven for all too brief a time.

The doctor walked over to Ben and gave him another hug. She said she knew she should go over to the shelter to volunteer but any contact with that odious place caused her despair. Ben could only nod to indicate that he knew and understood.

"We're still on for lunch Saturday, I hope. I've got to get my Ben Fix before I leave."

"Of course, although I wish you weren't going. I don't even want to know where." He was referring to her upcoming three-month tour with Doctors Without Borders.

"Better you don't" was the doctor's semi-sarcastic retort.

Walking toward the door, Ben took one last turn and quietly requested, "Please keep her here as long as you can."

# MARIE

# Chapter 4

"I hate this baby. She looks at me like she knows she isn't wanted." These harsh words were spoken by a fifteen year old who was certainly not prepared for motherhood.

"Why the hell did you go with that guy? You don't even know his name!"

"He was good looking and bought me things. I just wanted to have some fun. I'm tired of taking care of your brats all the time. Like you're so good, three fathers with three kids."

Thus went the conversation between mother and daughter. Despite the ravages of poverty, both of them were quite attractive. Marisol looked older than fifteen and had exquisite features. No doubt this had contributed to her plight. The father of her baby had no idea what a child she was.

She met him by a metro station. Marisol was on her way to her older sister's house on the other end of Queens to pick up hand-me-downs for the kids and for herself. Her sister had picked up several expensive outfits at a local resale shop, but she had put on quite a bit of weight lately, since she moved in with her boyfriend. Two babies and junk food will do it.

Marisol was wearing one of her sister's casts offs, a lovely brown check skirt coupled with an expensive looking beige blouse topped with a pale peach suede vest. High open-toed heels completed the picture. No stranger would ever suspect her vulnerable age.

It was the first time in weeks that Marisol had any free time to herself. She wasn't attending school, as she had to take care of her mother's three other children while she was at work; but today her mother was home due to illness. Instead of going directly to her sister's, Marisol took the subway up to Madison Avenue, where elegance blossomed and society's wealthy one percent thrived.

Marc, the CEO of a company that Forbes rated highly, had taken the afternoon off. He had rushed  home to pick up Lacy, his wife of eighteen years, and his two children and then dropped them off at the airport. They were going to visit Lacy's parents. Marc was glad he wasn't going along, since her parents had never trusted him.

He had to admit they had reason. Monogamy was not one of his strong points. He had already been caught cheating twice, but Lacy took him back both times. She didn't want to leave the cushy life they led, and he adored his children. Not seeing them daily would hurt.

Marc was going to stay in his apartment in the city, but he had no doubt that Lacy would call persistently to check on him. Thinking about the next three days, he knew that he would have to be cautious.

Marc glanced across the street and considered stopping at Porto's Bar for a drink. Crossing the street, he passed the high-end shoe store next to Porto's. Marc had paid many a bill from that boutique. Lacy loved that store and always managed to find a pair of Jimmy Choos or some other posh designer brand. That really didn't bother Marc, since money was not an issue.

The shoes didn't interest Marc, but the gorgeous number in front of the store piqued his interest. As she turned to walk away, she dropped a checked brown-and-peach scarf. Oblivious of her loss, she continued walking toward the subway.

Marc scooped up the scarf and slowly followed his prey until she was about to descend the subway steps. Not wanting to scare her, he tapped on her shoulder. Fearing the worst, she didn't turn around.

"Miss, I've been chasing you for blocks. You lost your scarf."

Marisol lived the high life that night. She called her mother and sister to cover her tracks and then rushed off for an evening with Marc, who had given her a false name. The fifteen year old didn't yet know that sweet words and passionate sex most often create no more than an ephemeral moment, certainly not the cement of a long-term relationship.

Marisol was not a virgin, which somewhat concealed her youth. Marc did fly the question of whether she was on the pill. Her quick response, "of course," erased his concern. Great sex can certainly dull caution. However, as the glow of dawn approached, her immaturity and lack of worldliness became apparent.

Marc determined to quickly cut ties with her. There was nothing to connect last night with his future. The hotel was not about to reveal his escapade. He did think about the credit card he had used, though. He dressed quickly and then tiptoeing over to the still sleeping form, he bent over to whisper good morning.

"I'm going out to get us some bagels."

Marisol's response was quite logical. "Just call Room Service."

To add plausibility, he said he also wanted to get a paper. Marc had plenty of experience with deception. Fifteen year olds believe what they want to. Marisol went right back to sleep. Marc went to the front desk to make sure his card had not yet been processed.

Telling the clerk he preferred to pay cash, Marc took enough money out of his wallet to cover the bill and a good-sized tip. He knew the clerk would pocket the tip and any connections with Marisol would vanish. Smiling as he walked back to his city apartment, he mused that one can have his cake and eat it too.

At 11 a.m., awakened by the knock at the door, Marisol jumped out of bed anticipating a few more hours with Marc. *Who knows,* she thought, *there may be more times like last night!*

Her fantasy was quickly burst as she opened the door. It was the maid notifying her that check out time was noon. Neither the bagels nor the romantic future had materialized.

Marisol left the hotel unaware that she was not alone. Still a child herself, a life was beginning within her.

# Chapter 5

Marisol dealt with her baby for three years. Beautiful hardly described this child. The deep violet shading of her eyes was mesmerizing. Coupled with her stunning looks, Marie was far above her years in intelligence. She read labels, signs, and words that helped her survive. The qualities that should have made her family proud did quite the opposite. They felt her accomplishments were "creepy."

Marisol's brother Paulo, who was in tenth grade, was the smartest of this dysfunctional family. He did well in school while causing no trouble. He kept his ambitions to himself, knowing they were alien to a family whose goals were almost non-existent.

Marie fascinated him. He wrote words and she had no trouble remembering them. He picked up books for her at a used book sale at school. At three, Marie could read a book comparable to *The Cat in the Hat* without previously seeing it.

Marisol worked for a nearby dry cleaners. Since her education had not reached beyond seventh grade, cleaning and pressing other people's clothes was her world. Her mother watched Marie while she was at work.

Anton, the owner's nephew, drove the cleaning van. Marisol's good looks and hot body were not lost on him. For her part, Marisol saw Anton as a way out of her dull existence.

After dating seriously for several months, the couple planned to get married. Marisol's mother encouraged this marriage. It certainly would give her daughter a step up from poverty. But Anton's family and friends all had negative responses, calling Marisol and her clan "lowlife." They also pointed out that marriage with her would include the burden of someone else's kid.

Anton began to have cold feet. As incredibly sexy as this girl was, maybe she wasn't the best long-term option for him.

"I don't want somebody else's kid in my house," the prospective groom blurted out at the end of an unpleasant evening.

His words scared Marisol. She felt the same way she had when Marc didn't come back to the hotel room. Hope for a better life was collapsing. Marie had always been a burden, and now she would ruin everything.

"Don't worry, Anton. My mother will take her."

"She better, or we're done."

Anton didn't offer to drive her home even though it was late, and Marisol's hands shook throughout the entire subway and bus ride home.

Climbing the dismal staircase to the apartment that had always been her home was like a prison sentence. Marisol knew her mother would never take Marie.

Dirty dishes were piled in the kitchen sink and soiled clothes filled a broken clothesbasket, waiting to be taken to the laundromat. Paulo was sitting at a table filled with bags of junk food trying to complete his homework. Her mother was watching television, half dozing, wearing the same baggy pants and top she had worn for the last two days.

Marie, in a stained shirt and pants too short for her growing legs, was coloring a sketch Paulo had designed. The precise care the little girl took to complete a complex drawing was most impressive. It turned Marisol's stomach to see evidence of the destruction of her life.

Marie accidently knocked over a glass of juice Paulo was drinking. Marisol flew over to her child and slapped her so hard she fell out of her chair and hit her head on Paulo's chair.

"What's the matter with you, Marisol? It was an accident," Paulo yelled at his sister while picking up Marie and examining her head.

"God, she's got a huge bump."

Marisol's anger rose when Marie didn't cry. The child's bravery sickened her.

Roused by the yelling, Marisol's mother got up from her chair to see what had happened. "What the hell is wrong with you, Marisol? Why do you always cause trouble?"

Marisol had little involvement with her daughter's care, except to contribute some of her salary to keep the family going. But now she realized she needed to cool it if she hoped to have her mother take full responsibility for Marie.

"Mom, I need to talk to you. Can we go into your room?"

Her mother's heart sank. She surmised there was trouble between Anton and her daughter, wiping out any hope that she might reap some benefits from the marriage. Anton's family was several rungs above them on the ladder of success.

Marisol's face paled as she blurted out her request. "Would you take Marie if Anton and I get married?"

"Are you out of your mind? I take care of her now just waiting for you to get married and go. I'm not going to take her to school and all the rest. I've done my share."

Paulo felt this was the biggest lie he had heard in a long time. His mother's contributions could be measured in a teaspoon and there would be lots of room left over. He felt badly for his little niece. He had a special bond with Marie. He was her only protector, and she loved him dearly.

"Mom, I'll take her to school in September and I'll take care of her now as much as I can."

"Hell no! The answer is no!"

Marisol offered her last plea. "Anton won't marry me if we have to take Marie."

The anger and fear that had built up within Marisol left no room for reason. She went into the room she shared with her younger sisters and Marie. After making sure the door was locked and blocked by a chair, she let her anger spill over as she emptied Marie's few items into a small cardboard suitcase. In another suitcase she packed two changes of clothes for herself. There was no place to hide the items in the tiny overcrowded room. She finally decided to make up a story and put the suitcases in another room.

She opened the door while trying to come up with something plausible. Her mother was immediately suspicious when she saw the suitcases.

# Chapter 6

"I'm going to take Marie over to Anton's and see if we can work something out."

That sounded so preposterous to Paulo that it frightened him as Marisol got ready to leave. He tried to persuade his sister to leave Marie with him, but that was not a solution for her.

Very quickly Marisol put a sweater on Marie and shoved her feet into her shoes. Marie apprehensively looked at her uncle for support. He was helpless because he was young and had no say. Marisol slammed the door with a vengeance and dragged Marie, whose small legs could not keep up, down the stairs.

They took the subway to a station where they could connect to a train that would take them out of town. As soon as the lights of the city faded, Marisol got off the train. In the darkness, she felt comfortable moving unnoticed. A group of people waited on the other side of the tracks. Obviously there wasn't much time before a return train would be departing for the city.

With all the passengers out on the platform, the station was empty. Marisol sat Marie down on a bench that was in the corner as far away from the ticket office as possible. Right now there was no one behind the desk.

"Someone nice will come and pick you up in a few minutes. But don't you ever mention our family's name or I will drown you."

Marie, young as she was, understood that she had to keep quiet as Marisol slipped out of the station and crossed to the platform on the other side. The sound of the approaching train meant there was little time to spare.

Now with only one suitcase and no child, Marisol felt a rush of emotions exploding like fireworks as thoughts of her new life made all this worthwhile. The one emotion missing was guilt.

The ringing of Anton's bell was music to her ears, but the lack of a response was a bit troubling. After bearing down on the bell several times, Marisol began banging on the door. She knew he was home because his truck was parked in the driveway. The noise brought nosy neighbors to their windows.

Anton finally answered the door, angry and disheveled. He was hardly the waiting lover. Pushing her way into the room, Marisol announced that Marie was no longer a problem.

The words barely left her lips when she noticed a woman with the barest of covering picking up a blouse from the floor next to the couch. Marisol had obviously interrupted something. Anton's first reaction was embarrassment, but then he quickly decided now was the time to get out of the marriage.

"Did you ever hear of phoning first?"

"I didn't think I had to," Marisol screamed hysterically. She dropped her small suitcase with such force that the cheap latches broke open, spilling the case's contents. Overwrought, she threw her purse across the small room, aiming it straight at the occupant of the couch. The girl, Maggie, had managed to get her blouse on and was now struggling into very tight pants.

Maggie's face was a perfect target for the flying missile with its metal latch. As the bag hit her mouth, blood spurted out, followed by three front teeth. Screaming in pain, Maggie flew out the door, leaving her teeth on the floor.

# Chapter 7

Marisol, blinded with rage and fear, bolted out the door. She had no idea what to do or where to go. Anton had just eliminated their future. Going home was not an option. She just knew she did not want to follow the same direction as Anton's girlfriend.

Unfortunately, the street she chose led to a warehouse terminal where trucks unloaded and then reloaded. Drivers were in a hurry to get in and out quickly. They didn't want to waste time waiting in line.

Marisol had no idea where she was. She ran haphazardly from side to side of the road. Meanwhile, an eighteen-wheeler left the highway, picking up speed as it headed for the terminal. The driver was distracted, looking for the entrance. Unaware that he had hit anything until he heard a sickening thud, he immediately glanced in the rear-view mirror and saw Marisol's crushed body stretched out behind his truck.

Since Marisol had no identification on her and no one actively searched for her, she became a Jane Doe. No one ever missed her since no one had been waiting for her.

# Chapter 8

While all this was taking place, Marie remained on the bench where
Marisol had placed her. The last train left the station at 10:15. Since
the stationmaster's job was finished, he quickly completed his closing
duties, flicked the lights off, locked the door, and headed home,
without ever seeing the three-year-old child huddled on a bench in
the corner.

Even though it was August, the evening night had a chill. Marie only
had the sweater Marisol had put on her. Pulling it more closely
around her, she curled up on the bench and fell asleep.

Before the sun was up on Saturday morning, the weekend ticket
agent arrived to begin his day. He immediately went to his desk to
look over the day's schedule, not even glancing at the benches.

Within minutes, a traveler discovered the little girl on the bench. The
ticket agent asked her question after question; but remembering
Marisol's threat, she divulged only her first name, age, and a few facts
that gave no clue about her family.

Some of the onlookers thought she was retarded, for certainly a three
year old would know something about where she lived. Far from
ignorant, Marie actually knew her address, apartment number, and
phone number, as well as Paulo's school's location and many of the
secrets of her dysfunctional family.

Many people who suffer mental or physical abuse want to go back to
their painful situation because at least it is familiar to them. Marie
never wanted to see Marisol again. She had absorbed all the hatred
her mother inflicted and desired no more. It was amazing for a three
year old to accept abandonment as being better than being with her
mother.

When the police arrived, Marie stuck to her story. One officer
remarked that he felt the child was not too swift. However, the

officer questioning Marie had years of experience with interrogations. He determined very quickly that this child was being secretive on purpose. He was reminded of the direction given to soldiers to prepare them in case they were captured by the enemy: "Just give your name, rank, and serial number."

Marie's unkempt appearance indicated neglect, and for that reason the officer felt her past should remain her past. Obviously she was not wanted. Why else would she be left to survive on her own? He filled out his report and phoned the local shelter.

The oddity of the whole situation was that Marie truthfully did not know her last name. The family was so dysfunctional that first names were all she had ever heard. At some point, someone suggested the name Eagan as a suitable last name, and so the child became Marie Eagan.

Marisol's family made no effort to search for her or her child. Her mother was happy to be rid of both of them. Eventually Paulo even stopped asking about Marie.

PJ Dischino

# CRAIG

# Chapter 9

Discord and abuse became a way of life for Mike and Sheila Farrow just two months after they had married. Their first child made her appearance four months later. By the time they'd been married six years, they had three children. Finally, Sheila made her way to Planned Parenthood and started taking the pill.

Mike's own problems were exacerbated by the steady drone of his nagging wife. Money was always at a premium in their household, since Mike's record of holding a job was slipshod at best. Jobs were plentiful for roofers, but Mike's quarrelsome encounters with bosses and coworkers contributed to his living on the edge.

Sheila worked for a cleaning service. She started work at 7 p.m. and got done at 3 a.m. She was home for the children during the day, but not really there. As soon as they were able to do anything for themselves, she left them on their own. At the age of five, each child was given a job that had to be done before there could be any playing.

Obviously love was not a sentiment expressed in the disenchanted Farrow family. The oldest child, Jennifer, resented her siblings because they became her responsibility. The two younger children hated her sour attitude and angry demands.

One afternoon, Sheila got a call from the school's social worker. The woman was very critical of the children's academic progress, as well as their appearance. By the end of the call, a dreaded home appointment had been set up, even though the social worker felt there was little hope for change.

Sheila had just gotten off the phone when her best friend, Angel, called and asked if she wanted to go out for a drink. It wasn't the first time the two friends had gone partying. Sheila would call in sick but would let Mike think she was at work; then she wouldn't have to be home until after three in the morning. The kids were asleep at that time and Mike was usually oblivious. At least twice a week Mike rolled home from work smelling of bars and, at times, perfume. He had to be home in time for Sheila to leave for work, although he didn't even look at the children.

On these evenings his loveless demand for sex before she had to leave for work made her brief outings with Angel all the more exciting. She also knew Mike found solace in various female encounters.

Faithfulness, respect, and even the least bit of tenderness were non-existent in their marriage. Mike would kill her if he found out she was sleeping around, not because he felt any affection for her but because he believed she was his possession.

Recently even their brief bedroom encounters had stopped. Mike's new girlfriend required little material rewards. She seemed content to spend a few hours on her couch with Mike, considering him quite the hunk.

Since Sheila and Angel were both married, they did their partying twenty-five miles away, where the city lights were bright and they could live it up without being caught. Sheila was still quite attractive as vanity kept her more worried about her figure than the welfare of her children. She dressed attractively but not overly seductively, although her black dress trimmed with tiny seed pearls at the neckline did nothing to hide her shapely figure.

They stayed at the first club, the Happy Hour, for just a short time. The patrons were all under thirty, and their immature conversations coincided with their callow youth.

"Let's try an upscale club," Angel suggested.

"I don't have much to spend at a ritzy place," Sheila responded.

"Don't worry. We'll nurse a glass of white wine for ages. Let's try the Bedford. That's about as topnotch as you can get. We can see how the other half lives."

The expense of a taxi was unthinkable so they walked the ten blocks to their destination wearing high heels. Nursing blisters by the time they arrived, they both felt like kicking off their shoes; but going into a posh hotel carrying your shoes wasn't very stylish. They laughed as they pictured that scene. Being free for an evening gave them a sense of giddiness.

The hotel was a vision with its glamorous marble lobby luring wealthy guests in for a high-end experience. They walked into the cocktail lounge with an air of belonging and sat at a high table where they could see the action and maybe be a part of it. In order to make a glass of wine last for an hour, they would have to take tiny and infrequent sips.

While the two friends didn't feel outclassed, they did feel unnoticed since most of the partygoers were in groups. The evening that had started with anticipation of some fun was fizzling out. Each woman wore a look of sheer boredom. Sheila got up first, pushing her chair in and suggesting they leave for home even though it was only 10:30. She wasn't looking forward to walking to the bus station in those dreaded heels.

Angel was still sitting at the table, not quite ready for the return hike. "Come on, let's stay just a few more minutes. I'm going to order another wine before I walk on these killers."

"Fine, Angel, maybe the wine will help."

The two sipped their second glass as they passed the time. Sheila mentioned the social worker at the kids' school who had threatened there might be some kind of intervention if the children kept coming to school unkempt, tired, and unprepared. "Shit on her. What does she know about marriage or kids? She's not even married," Sheila whined.

Angel nodded in agreement. "Why the hell did we ever get married?"

"We were stupid and the sex was good," Sheila sighed.

# Chapter 10

Suddenly, things got a little more interesting. A couple sitting at the bar was having a heated conversation. Their exchange shot up a few decibels as the barbs flew back and forth. Soon the caustic remarks morphed into a full-fledged argument, ending with the woman slapping her companion and leaving the bar without looking back.

Angel, who had been facing the couple, reported that the guy was gorgeous but told Sheila not to turn around. However, the man had already caught a glimpse of Sheila in her stunning black sheath when he entered the bar.

The fight with his fiancée riled him. The fact that they both came from good families and had status jobs didn't hide the fact that they had little in common besides their money. Jonathan was ready for a diversion, and that pretty woman could fill the bill.

He told the bartender to send over two glass of Cristal champagne to the ladies, pointing to Sheila and Angel with his eyes. The women raised the crystal flutes to the generous gentleman. Although they had never tasted Cristal before, the look Sheila gave the handsome man as she raised her glass to him implied that although this was a lovely gesture it was nothing out of the ordinary.

Angel quickly determined that "three is a crowd."

"Sheila, I'm going to take off. Will that work for you?"

"Thanks. You're a doll, Angel."

After emptying the last drop from her flute, Angel got up and slowly sauntered out of the lounge.

As soon as she was gone, Jonathan walked over to Sheila's table and asked if he could join her. Sheila nodded as she noted his striking good looks: blond hair and green eyes with deep, gorgeous dimples when he smiled.

The conversation was heavily one-sided. Craig, the phony name Jonathan gave Sheila, rambled on about a few subjects. His complaints about the woman who had been his companion occupied much of the conversation. That proved to be a bonus, since Sheila didn't want to talk about herself and her joyless existence. Her nods to the points Craig made, along with her words of sympathy and support, lifted Craig's doldrums. Here was someone who listened and didn't nag.

After they had talked for a while, Craig excused himself, telling Sheila he would be right back. Once he was out of view, her spirits plunged. He was probably not coming back. She had five dollars left in her purse.

It was after 11:00 when Sheila reached for her purse, knocking over the empty flute. Tears filled her eyes as another crisis spoiled the evening. The broken crystal matched her disillusionment.

"Don't get so upset. It's only a glass. I'll take care of it. I'm sorry I was so long."

Someone had thrown her a life preserver.

During his absence, Craig had reserved the penthouse suite. He was that confident that Sheila would join him. He reasoned that she did not want to divulge details about her life, and neither did he. So why pass up an evening of pleasure with no strings?

"Would you consider joining me in my room here to continue a very lovely evening? You have brightened my day. We could have something to eat. How does that sound?"

Having a taste of luxury, even short-lived, was so appealing that Sheila disregarded any potential negative consequences. Even the elevator with its built-in television dazzled her.

Once they were in the suite, Craig suggested they order a steak. Sheila, overwhelmed by the view of the city from the twenty-third floor, nodded dreamily and replied, "Sounds wonderful." She heard him ordering Chateaubriand, an item that had not appeared on any menu she had ever seen.

Soon a beautifully detailed cart was rolled into the room, set with silver, crystal, and china. The large, perfectly grilled steak surrounded by roasted vegetables definitely was an improvement over the Hamburger Helper she usually had for dinner!

Sheila didn't care how short this affair would be. It was giving her a brief escape from her cheerless life.

Not realizing that the two had fallen asleep after passionate lovemaking, Sheila was yanked back to reality when the phone rang. The call was for Craig. Sheila looked over at the clock. It was 3 a.m., the time she was supposedly leaving her job. She was dressed before Craig had finished his call.

"I have to pee. Don't leave before I come back," Craig said in an annoyed tone.

Sheila had no idea what his problem was. Maybe it had to do with the phone call, but she couldn't care less. The time and having no money to get home were her only concerns.

As soon as Craig went into the bathroom, Sheila rushed toward the bedroom door to leave. As she passed the night stand next to his side of the bed, she noticed a wad of bills. She picked up the bundle, terror-stricken she would be caught. After opening the folded wad and grabbing the bottom bill, she returned the money to its original spot and quickly made her exit. As she closed the door, she heard the flush of the toilet.

She ran down the steps to the next floor and then waited for the elevator. It took an eternity before the doors opened. When she got to the lobby, she walked quickly out the same door she and Angel had entered a few hours before.

She looked at the hundred dollar bill in her hand. It might be enough to take a taxi home. She questioned the lone taxi driver parked near the hotel's entrance. Seventy-five dollars was his fee.

Arriving home, Sheila carefully turned the key in the door, hoping Mike was asleep. He would certainly question her if he saw the outfit she was wearing. It was not something she wore home after her cleaning jobs.

Thankfully, the house was dark and quiet. Sheila stripped off all evidence of her rendezvous and shoved everything into the clothes basket, where no one else would look. Slipping into bed next to Mike, Sheila marveled at how well she had pulled off such a crazy stunt. However, just before she closed her eyes, Sheila remembered a frightening fact that made sleep impossible.

She and Mike had not made love since his liaison with his new catch. Last month she had not refilled her birth control pills because she was broke. No matter how drunken Mike was, any chance of pregnancy usually froze his sexual desire. Now she would have to undergo a few weeks of sweating it out before she knew if her little adventure would have any negative consequences.

# Chapter 11

Sheila was relieved when Mike woke up in the morning and reached over to fondle her breasts. He was pleasantly surprised at his wife's warm reaction. Sheila was covering all her bases.

The ensuing days clouded her lovely fling. The worry of a pregnancy never let up. She hated every time she was pregnant. Abortion wasn't an option. It was not a religious thing for her, though it was for Mike. However, Sheila had a deathly fear of any kind of medical attention. Health issues were often neglected until a crisis necessitated emergency attention. Once her son almost died because of his mother's neglect, coupled with her fear of doctors. He was complaining of stomach distress, even crying at times, and finally ended up in the emergency room with a burst appendix.

The month dragged on. Sheila berated herself daily for her pill debacle. Finally, she recognized the early signs of pregnancy. It took another month of stalling before she blurted it out when she and Mike were alone.

"For Christ sake, I thought you were on the pill!"

Sheila made up an excuse that she had used pills that were years old as she had forgotten to get a new prescription. She also added that she had to see a doctor before her prescription could be refilled. Mike accepted that story since he knew her phobia about anything or anybody attached to the field of medicine.

Having another mouth to feed was the last thing Mike expected or wanted. He certainly would spend more time with his friends and girlfriend now. He wasn't going to hang around listening to another screaming brat.

Mike became a passive member of the household and his absences increased. This did not upset Sheila one bit. It did affect the children. The social worker threatened to call in the health department as well as child welfare. The children appeared neglected when they were at school, and their attendance was spotty. The social worker cringed when Sheila's pregnancy grew obvious.

Cleaning offices drained her as her heavy body tried to keep up with the daily routine. Normally a woman finds joy with her part in the development of a new life. Sheila felt no love for her unborn child, just a deep resentment.

Angel was the only one privy to the truth. She truly felt empathetic with her friend's plight. Her own marriage was no bargain. Once when the two were able to get together, Angel tried to add a little levity to their gloomy conversations by blurting out, "God Sheila, what if that baby has your dream man's gorgeous looks?" As soon as the words came out, Angel realized this could be a tragic joke.

Perhaps Sheila's mind was protecting her from more anxiety, but that had never entered her mind. She and Mike both had brown hair and brown eyes. Their children had brown hair and brown eyes. Craig was blond and his eyes were green.

From that moment on, terror consumed her entire being. Her fear didn't help her deal with everyday life. Her belligerent attitude caused people to keep her at arm's length.

When Sheila delivered the baby, Angel was the only one with her. Mike couldn't be found. Actually, that was a relief to Sheila. She would be the first to see the baby's features. She had a recurring dream that the baby had Craig's adult head.

To add to Sheila's distress, this baby gave her unbelievable agony for hours. Finally it was determined that the baby's position was a problem and she would need a Caesarian.

Sheila hoped that this baby would be born dead. That would solve all her problems. But as the doctor lifted it from her body, she heard him say, "You should be so proud. You have a perfect baby boy."

Sheila was so exhausted she could barely focus until something drew her out of her fog. It was the expression on Angel's face when she first saw the baby. It did not bode well.

Sheila reasoned to herself, *All newborns look somewhat alike, so everything is fine for now.* That theory was quashed when the nurse brought over her baby. It was as if her unfaithfulness was now being exposed to the world.

The baby was as perfect as any newborn could be. Most mothers would be enthralled with his fair skin and beautifully shaped features. Sheila looked at him as if he were an alien creature. This child would be her downfall. He was the image of Craig. Like all newborns, his eyes were a dark blue. If they changed to green in a few months, she would certainly be doomed. Two brown-eyed parents do not have a green-eyed baby.

Sheila had to take reasonable care of the baby, as the social worker would just pop in without warning, especially since there was an infant in the home now. Sheila named him Craig out of spite, not knowing the father's name was really Jonathan. That one night of glory had certainly backfired on her.

The two youngest Farrow children couldn't care less about this newcomer. Jenny, the oldest, hated her younger siblings. It was certainly understandable, as she was the one who usually had to take care of their needs. She fed them, gave them baths, and did their laundry. These were chores that no young girl should have to take on.

But Jenny was fascinated by Craig. He was like a beautiful doll. When no one was looking, she offered him her fingers, which he grabbed with his beautiful long ones. He smiled at her when given the least amount of attention.

Within a few days, Craig had won Jenny's heart. As soon as she got home from school, she rushed over to him, changed his diaper, and gave him a bottle while singing a song or just telling him about her day. He, in turn, responded with pure joy.

Jenny observed things about this baby that surprised her. Craig looked nothing like anyone in the family; and when he was four months old, Jenny noticed that his eyes were turning green. She also noted that his motor skills were far ahead of her friend's baby sister. She was just able to roll over while Craig could sit up.

Angel stopped over one afternoon. She hadn't seen her friend in several weeks. Sheila wasn't home, and Angel couldn't help noticing that Jenny and Craig were totally entertained by each other. Jenny was happy with this baby, which shocked Angel. Normally, Jenny was sullen and defiant and looked disheveled and unkempt. However, her whole appearance had changed. She had washed and combed her hair and was wearing a clean, though faded, blouse and skirt.

Jenny talked away about Craig, about how smart he was and how he loved her. Angel was amazed when Jenny showed her how Craig could sit up and how he laughed at every playful word Jenny uttered.

When Angel remarked how beautiful and smart Craig was, Jenny's face lit up with pride. It was as if she were his mother. Then she turned to Angel and pointed out what she had discovered a few days ago, that Craig's eyes were turning green.

Shock waves rolled through Angel's body. She quickly asked Jenny if her mother had noticed that his eyes were changing. The girl shrugged and said her mom really didn't pay much attention to Craig. When she's wasn't working, her mom was in her room drinking or sleeping. The lady next door took care of Craig while Jenny was at school.

Angel asked about Jenny's dad. Jenny told her Mike wasn't home most of the time. When he was, he barely acknowledged the older children and never bothered to look at Craig.

Jenny paused and then, with tears welling up in her eyes, began to tell Angel about the social worker's frequent visits. She had told Sheila that if the neglect continued, the children would be taken away.

Their conversation was interrupted when Sheila walked in. She and Angel spoke for a few minutes after Jenny took the baby into the bedroom. When Angel mentioned Craig's eyes, Sheila became agitated.

"Oh my God. I knew the baby looked like Craig as soon as he was born, but I figured that Mike wouldn't really pay much attention to him so I could still pass the baby off as his. But the eyes—I was worried about the eyes changing! Those green eyes will be a dead giveaway to Mike that the baby isn't his. God knows what he'll do to me when he discovers the truth!"

Brushing past Angel, Sheila burst into the bedroom, where Jenny was getting Craig ready for bed. Blind with rage and fear, she snatched the half-dressed infant out of Jenny's arms with such force that he started to scream uncontrollably. Carrying him over to the lamp, she screeched at Jenny to switch it on to the brightest setting. By now the baby was crying so hard that she could barely see his eyes at all.

Then she actually let go of the baby. If Jenny hadn't been standing right next to her, he would have fallen on the floor. Although Jenny was terrified, she had the presence of mind to grab the baby, rush into the bathroom, and lock the door. She knew that she would have to calm down herself if she hoped to quiet Craig. Softly, she began to sing. At first it was half song, half sob, but eventually her singing became sweeter and Craig's screams turned into whimpers. Jenny sang and rocked Craig gently until he finally fell asleep.

Angel knocked softly on the door and asked Jenny to let her in. Cautiously, Jenny opened the door slightly and peeked out. Satisfied that Angel was alone, Jenny quickly pulled her inside and then shut and locked the door again.

"Your mother is asleep. I think she has really gone off the deep end. I don't know what to tell you, but I don't think it's safe here."

Angel didn't offer to bring the children home with her. Her husband would have a fit if she got involved. She really just wanted to take off before Mike got home. Telling Jenny to take the kids next door, she quickly made her own getaway.

Jenny knew she couldn't just stay in that bathroom. She opened the door, making as little noise as possible. The two younger kids were crouched in the corner of the bedroom, too frightened to cry. She grabbed blankets and diapers before tiptoeing into the kitchen to grab the bottles she had prepared when she'd gotten home from school.

As she was stuffing everything into a shopping bag, her younger brother jumped up and ran over to her. Tugging at her skirt, he desperately begged, "Don't leave me, Jenny. Please don't leave me."

After reassuring him that she wouldn't leave him, Jenny handed him two shopping bags and whispered, "Get your sister, go into the bedroom, and fill these bags with as many clothes as you can. Make sure you bring sweaters. As soon as you finish, go out the front door and wait for me."

# Chapter 12

The terrified children gathered on the front porch. Following Angel's advice, Jenny took them next door to Craig's babysitter. One of the women's sullen children opened the door. Fifteen-year-old Cal Reston had the reputation of being a bully and had been suspended from school for starting fights and beating up younger kids.

Scared but desperate, Jenny begged in a shaky voice, "Please help us, Cal."

Normally, Cal would have laughed at Jenny and called her a whiner. But staring into the wide eyes of the three trembling children on his doorstep spooked Cal. The bully ran into the house, screaming for his mother. Shocked to hear fear in her son's voice, she rushed to the front door.

"Please let us in. We're in awful trouble," Jenny pleaded.

Cal's mother, Lois, quickly ushered the children into the living room, where an unwatched television was blaring the news. Within a few minutes, all the members of her family were gathered in the living room to find out what was going on. In a barely audible voice, Jenny told them what had happened.

Lois felt sorry for the children, but at the same time a mental red flag told her not to get in the middle of a domestic argument. Over the years, she and the other neighbors had overheard more than a few of Mike's unprovoked rages directed at his family.

Bringing the Farrow children into the kitchen, Lois gave them cookies and milk while she and her husband went back to the living room to discuss the situation.

Five minutes later, Lois came back into the kitchen and spoke to Jenny. "I'm so sorry for you and your family. I know what happened has been very scary for you kids and I know you need help. Jenny, you are just too young to be responsible for yourself and the rest of the children. I've talked it over with my husband. We'd like to help you, but we also have to make sure that our own kids are safe. It wouldn't be a good idea for us to get in the middle of your parents' problems. So we're going to call the police to help us. They'll know what to do and will make sure you kids are safe."

Jenny didn't even respond. In her mind, there was no solution to her problem.

Lois' husband, John, called 911 and explained the situation with their neighbors. When he got off the phone, he told Jenny that the police would be there soon.

Help couldn't come fast enough for Lois. She didn't know what would happen when Sheila or Mike discovered the children were missing. She just wanted to be sure she and her family weren't involved.

The police took the children to the station and notified Family Services. They would work with Sheila's social worker to make arrangements for the children until an assessment of their home situation could be made.

Lois felt a little guilty yet relieved to have the Farrow children out of her home. By calling the police and turning the kids over to them, she had averted a potentially dangerous situation with Mike. Who knew what kind of rage he might fly into once he realized his family was gone? Yet she couldn't get the faces of those children out of her mind.

Even Cal was affected by the situation. Alone in his room, he finally stopped trying to hold back his tears. The fake bravado had disappeared, and for the first time in his life, he genuinely felt sorry for someone besides himself.

If there was anything positive to come out of this, it was the complete metamorphosis in Cal's character. He stopped making sarcastic and nasty comments. He became a giver, not a taker. His grades improved. He often cried inwardly as the vision of Jenny's desperation, and his inability to help her haunted him. He pledged to himself that when he became an adult, he would find her and protect her forever.

# Chapter 13

The Farrow children were, unfortunately, separated from each other. Jenny was placed in a few different foster homes but eventually ended up with a gracious, loving couple. She had applied herself at school and received a scholarship to college. In addition, she worked part-time in an office and started to save a little money. After graduation she was offered a teaching job in a town 300 miles away.

Once she was settled in a little apartment of her own, Jenny began the search for her lost siblings. In less than a year, she located her younger sister, who was happily married with a brand new baby girl that she had named Jenny.

Next, she received news about her first brother. He had joined the army and been killed in Iraq. The memory of the little boy tugging on her skirt and pleading, "Please don't leave me!" lingered with Jenny. She would always regret that she hadn't made any attempt to love or care for him before that day.

The deepest and most painful ache of all had been the loss of Craig, her precious baby brother. All her efforts to track him down had failed. It was as if he had never existed.

The phone rang early one evening while Jenny was feeding her cat, Lizzie. A man with an unfamiliar male voice asked to speak to Jenny Farrow.

"This is Cal Reston, Jenny. You are without a doubt the hardest person to find. I've been at this for years."

The name certainly wasn't one she ever wanted to hear again. She remembered what a big bully he had been. They had nothing in common but bad memories. Why would he spend years looking for her?

Cal told her that he finally found her thanks to a newspaper article his mother had sent him announcing she had been named Teacher of the Year.

Jenny laughed to herself. Cal, of all people, had tracked her down. Why couldn't it have been Craig who found her?

Cal said he would be in her area to attend his father's funeral and asked if he could meet her. Jenny didn't offer her condolences or even ask where Cal was living now. In a flat voice, she pointed out that she lived three hundred miles from his family home.
Jenny didn't want to be rude, but she had no interest in seeing Cal or reliving painful memories. "Cal, I have no interest in going back to that time. I don't see any purpose in our meeting. Let's just leave it at that."

"Jenny, I understand exactly how you feel. I just want to see you to make sure you're okay and happy. I'm not that boy you remember. Give me a chance. I don't want to add more hurt to your life. My family actually lives in Sheffield, which isn't far from where you are now. My mom saw the article about you in the local paper."

When Cal mentioned Sheffield, Jenny realized his family lived less than fifteen miles from her. She often worked with teachers from that town on county projects. She wondered if he had changed. His tone was sincere, and the cockiness seemed gone. If she met him at a public location, she could just leave if things didn't go well. And maybe, just maybe, he might know something about what had happened to Craig.

Jenny told him to call when he had time and maybe they could meet for lunch. Cal said he'd check in with her when he could get away for a few hours.

Two days later, Cal called. He had several hours before his father's evening visitation at the funeral home so he wondered if she could meet him for lunch. He had taken a chance that she would say yes and made a reservation at Bransons. Jenny gulped when she heard his choice. The posh restaurant was definitely out of her price range.

Recalling that his parents had been living in Sheffield, an affluent town with spectacular homes framed by picture-perfect landscapes, Jenny could only assume that somehow the family had come into some money.

Jenny and Cal actually had a wonderful time at lunch. Cal was no longer an overweight, slovenly boy. Amazingly, he had morphed into a handsome, well-dressed young man with a crinkly smile and a quick wit. And Jenny had transformed from a sad and forlorn little girl into a self-assured woman who was both beautiful and intelligent.

That evening Jenny attended the visitation for Cal's father and was surprised to see a long line of mourners streaming into the funeral home to pay their last respects. She wouldn't have expected such a large turnout for the foreman of a town's road crew.

Even though many years had passed, Jenny was sure she would recognize Cal's mother, whom she remembered as a shapeless, sloppy dresser who never smiled. But Jenny didn't recognize anyone in the group of impeccably dressed people surrounding Cal. She was confused when Cal turned to a stylish middle-aged woman and announced, "Mom, here she is."

Enfolding Jenny in her arms, the woman exclaimed, "Oh Jenny, you've been in our thoughts ever since that horrible night. And when our ship sailed in, we began to search for you. For years we had no luck, until the day I saw the article about you in the newspaper."

Jenny mentioned that a fire in one of the shelters had destroyed most of the records, though there were copies of some in the state archives. She herself had invested as much time and money as she could to track down her family. She briefed Lois about what had happened to her younger sister and brother but explained that she could find no record at all of a baby named Craig Farrow.

Lois invited Jenny back to the house after the visitation. "An army couldn't finish all the food that neighbors and friends have dropped off. Is it possible for you to stay overnight? There's plenty of room and there is so much to catch up on. We'd all love for you to stay.

Tomorrow's going to be a terrible day." Jenny squeezed her hand as tears welled up in the older woman's eyes.

Tomorrow was Saturday, so Jenny accepted the invitation with grace. After leaving the funeral home, she rushed home to feed the cat and quickly pack a bag. When she pulled up to the Reston house, Jenny felt a bit nervous about going inside. What was she doing? A part of her felt that these people were strangers to her—very nice people but nothing like the family she had known. And yet there were so many shared memories from her childhood. Cal was so different from that taunting bully of so long ago, and Jenny felt attracted to him. She saw only kindness and charm in him now. And it didn't hurt that he was good looking to boot! She decided she had nothing to lose, so she got out of her car, walked up the stairs to the huge Tudor style home, and rang the bell.

Jenny could not get over the house, which was tastefully decorated with comfy, overstuffed chairs, lush draperies, and leather couches. The dining room overlooked a well-manicured lawn with clusters of day lilies, hostas, and begonias. A rose garden had been planted in the middle of the yard, and the pink, lavender, crimson, and soft yellow bushes gushed with blooms.

# Chapter 14

After they had finished eating, the group gathered in the living room to spend some time reflecting about everything that had happened during the past few days. To Jenny, the contrast between today and the last time they had been together was incredible. It was hard to believe these were the same boorish, uncharitable people whose fear of getting involved had been responsible for her being separated from her siblings.

After everyone had chosen a spot to sit and settled in, one of Cal's sisters broached the subject that everyone in her family had been wondering about—what had happened to Jenny and her siblings after the police took them away? Was the family kept together? Were they adopted? Where were they now?

Cal knew a bit about what had happened and how painful it was for Jenny to discuss, so he suggested that maybe they should update Jenny on what had been happening with them before they all ganged up on her. After all, there were several of them and only one of her!

Jenny thought this would be a great time to find out how the Restons had been able to change their lifestyle so drastically. Laughing softly, she remarked, "You know, since I met Cal for lunch I've become more and more curious about what's happened to your family. How were you able to get out of the old neighborhood and end up in a magnificent home like this?"

"Jenny, you poor baby. We didn't realize you had no idea how we escaped from that old hovel. We assumed Cal had told you our story," Cal's sister replied.

"My only clue was your mom's remark about your ship coming in."

"Hmmm, sounds intriguing, doesn't it? So what do you think happened?"

Jenny shook her head and then shrugged, finally asking if they had found the pot of gold at the end of the rainbow. They all chuckled, and then Cal said it didn't quite happen that way but she was pretty close. He gave her a hint—it was one word. Jenny guessed *inheritance.* This time everyone laughed out loud.

"There isn't any money in any branch of our family tree," Cal explained.

"It's really a great story," Lois began. "I was doing my grocery shopping at the A & P and had just finished paying the cashier when I ran into a woman I knew. She immediately apologized for not paying back the five dollars she'd borrowed the week before. She had promised to pay it back the same day but then had never gotten back to me. I'd been a little peeved since I really couldn't afford to be out five dollars.

"The woman immediately fished around in her purse and pulled out a five dollar bill. I could tell she was embarrassed as she handed me the money, so I tried to be gracious as I accepted it. But since I'd already finished shopping, the money was a little late. I don't know what possessed me because I'd never done this before, but as I walked out of the store I stopped at customer service and bought a Mega Million lottery ticket.

"When I got home, I put the ticket in my dresser drawer and quickly forgot about it. The next week I noticed a headline in the paper announcing that a local single ticket had won the Mega Million lottery but that no one had claimed it.

"Rushing into the bedroom with the paper in my hand, I yanked the dresser draw open and routed around for the ticket. Sure enough, when I compared my ticket to the number in the paper, it was a match!"

What a wild story! Jenny would never have believed it if she hadn't seen the "before" and now the "after" with her own eyes.

# Chapter 15

The funeral for John Reston was by far the largest the town had ever experienced. What separated the Restons from other newly rich families were their priorities. Their lifestyle was one of luxury but not blatantly ostentatious. John and Lois had been quite generous with their good fortune, dedicating their lives to philanthropic endeavors; and their children chose careers in which they could serve society and make a difference.

A favorite charity was a hospital wing they had funded that was dedicated to children who had been abandoned or removed from their homes due to abuse or neglect. Although they had searched for Jenny for years, all their attempts had led them to a dead end. But she was always in their thoughts, and so they named the hospital wing "Jennifer's Outreach."

The Restons had done so much for the community and now the grateful citizens, as well as friends and neighbors, turned out to express their gratitude and respect for John. After the funeral, the family invited everyone back to their home to share a meal and memories of Mr. Reston.

John's favorite restaurant had catered a magnificent Italian meal of fettuccine, eggplant parmesan, antipasto salad, and crusty garlic bread, as well as cannoli shells with a creamy, rich ricotta filling. The spread was already laid out on a buffet table when the guests arrived. Cal and his two younger sisters mingled with the guests, sharing favorite stories about their father. Although there were moments of sadness, there were far more chuckles and smiles shared that afternoon.

When all the guests were gone, the family once again gathered in the living room. After hearing about the family's compassion and the generosity they had demonstrated in the community, as well as the hospital wing dedicated to her, Jenny's opinion of the Restons had completely reversed. She decided it was time to tell them what had happened to her family after the police took them away that night so long ago.

Jenny was dazed during the ride to the station, the questioning, and the final transfer of the children to some sort of shelter. They were surrounded by several people, but Jenny couldn't focus on anything but Craig, refusing to let anyone near him. When Craig began to cry uncontrollably, a uniformed lady kindly offered to feed him and then bring him back to Jenny. The young girl was so exhausted by now that she gratefully agreed to let the woman take Craig away. The last thing she remembered was telling the woman the bottles were in the paper bag next to her.

Twenty-four hours later, Jenny awakened in an unfamiliar bedroom. She called out for Craig, and someone assured her there was nothing to worry about—everything was under control. Jenny smiled weakly before her fatigue pulled her down into the darkness of sleep once again.

When she fully awoke the following morning, anxiety and fear consumed her. She had to know what had happened to her siblings. Running out of her room, she was confused to find herself in a larger, empty room. She panicked and started to cry, yelling for someone to come and help her. Finally two women rushed into the room.

"Where are my brothers and sister? What have you done with them? I want to see them immediately!" Jenny demanded. By now she was hysterically screaming and stomping her feet on the floor. One of the women hurriedly left the room, returning with a huge, muscular man who whisked Jenny up in his arms and plopped her back onto the bed. Jenny quieted down quickly but would not stop begging for information.

"You are all wards of the court now," one of the women finally responded. "We can't handle infants here, so your baby brother was sent to a special facility. The other two have been transferred to other less-crowded shelters."

"You don't even know their names. You've taken the baby away from me, and I'm the only one he knows and loves. You're tearing our family apart, and you don't even know or care about us!"

Once again overcome with hysterics, Jenny carried on until exhaustion finally took over and her mind went numb. After that, she stopped fighting and let them sedate her.

After spending a week in a hospital, Jenny was transported to a new facility.

# Chapter 16

A "perfect storm" of errors was the cause of a four-month-old infant's loss of identity. One of the policeman who drove the children to the station was late to relieve his wife so she could get to work. In a hurry, he scribbled his record of the incident on a sticky note attached to an empty folder. He assumed his partner was going to make the official report and submit it in the morning. His partner picked up the folder and took it along to the shelter where he took the Farrow children later that night. Without thinking, he left it on the desk there. The attendant's shift was about to end, so she left the folder for the next attendant coming on duty.

By the time the new shift was in full swing, all of the Farrow children except Jenny had been transferred to separate facilities. The baby had been sent to a special home just for infants and toddlers that was located seventy-five miles away.

And so Craig arrived at his new "home" with a folder labeled Nicholas Garlow. The admitting attendant noticed a scribbled sticky note attached to the folder. Figuring the almost illegible note was unimportant, she threw it in the garbage, never thinking to read it first. If she had checked, she would have discovered that the name on the note didn't match the name on the folder. Nicholas Garlow was actually the name of the custodian at the children's school. The poor man had died a few days earlier. Since he had no family, the town collected money to give him a simple burial.

Before the age of digital record keeping, files were frequently misplaced, mislabeled, or misfiled. As a result of this error, it seemed that Craig Farrow never existed. A few years later, a fire destroyed the building and all the records, so the mistake was never discovered or corrected. No one would have ever guessed that Nicholas Garlow was really Craig Farrow.

Over the years, Jenny had stayed with a few different foster families, but somehow she always found herself back at the orphanage. One of the doctors who volunteered there took an interest in her. Hidden beneath her lack of self-esteem, he discovered an exceptionally gifted and intelligent girl. Dr. Jamison was well aware of the hopeless path her life could take when she left the home at seventeen. He wondered if there was anything he could do to help her avoid a life of despair.

Once Dr. Jamison asked Jenny if she ever remembered a time when she was happy. Tears immediately welled up in her eyes, but he detected a slight glimmer there as well. After some encouragement, Jenny described her wonderful four months with her baby brother.

The doctor realized the two had a very special connection of pure love. But when Craig was taken away, that bond was destroyed, and so was Jenny. Feeling hopeless, Jenny retreated within herself. Building on this revelation, the doctor often encouraged Jenny to apply herself at school so that she could get a good job when she grew up and then she could search for Craig

When Dr. Jamison was close to seventy, he finally considered the possibility of retirement. His wife, Carrie, had been pleading with him to retire for the past five years. Carrie wanted to have more time with her husband. They were a loving couple who always thought of each other first, but Carrie had felt lonely over the years since they never had any children. She'd spent enough years being a doctor's wife and sharing Jim with his patients. She was determined to spend more time with him in their senior years.

As Jim's retirement approached, he worried more and more about Jenny. She would finish high school next year and would no longer be a ward of the state. But she was totally unprepared for life outside of an institution. There had been such improvement in her in academics and in her self-confidence, but he didn't think she'd continue her growth without support.

If he didn't have Carrie to consider, he would take it upon himself to create a safe and supportive environment for Jenny. But that certainly wouldn't be fair to the woman he loved. Her plans for their retirement and the opportunity to travel and spend more time together certainly didn't include taking care of a teen who would still need a great deal of guidance and support for the next few years. At least that's what Jim assumed.

Carrie knew all about Jenny, since Jim had been telling her about the girl for years. She also knew her husband had helped Jenny to slowly come out of her depression. Now she actually had hope that she might be reunited with her younger brother one day.

Finally, Jim could no longer keep his concerns to himself. During one of their conversations about Jenny's future, he just blurted out how worried he was about her. This was the opportunity Carrie had been waiting for. After sharing her own concerns about Jenny's well-being, Carrie presented Jim with a plan to help the girl. Jim was amazed when his wife suggested they take Jenny in as a foster child.

Jim was still concerned that this would be too much of a sacrifice. It meant putting their travel plans on hold for another year or so, until Jenny could function on her own. He also worried because Jenny wasn't the most pleasant company when she suffered one of her bouts with depression. During these times, guilt over her neglect of her brother and sister overwhelmed her. And the loss of baby Craig haunted her, throwing her into a perpetual state of mourning. Dr. Jamison had partially broken through that hopeless cloud by encouraging Jenny to work hard in school, suggesting she might get a scholarship to college. But he wanted his wife to be aware of all the baggage Jenny brought along with her.

Carrie understood the extent of effort required. In her heart Carrie understood that lending a helping hand was a part of life. She was offering a gift of love to a man who had served the world of medicine with dedication and devotion. His fidelity as well as his endearing love for her never took a break. How could anything be a sacrifice?

It turned out not to be a sacrifice at all. For a few weeks the situation was touchy. A wall of misery doesn't dismantle easily. Jenny didn't expect Carrie to have the same tender concern for her as Dr. Jim had. But even though she came into Jenny's life later, Carrie became the mother figure Jenny sorely missed.

The ice began to melt. Jenny came alive and started to let some joy into her life. She attended a nearby college on a scholarship, even though she'd also had scholarship offers from a few better known schools. The Jamisons encouraged her to look into all her choices, but Jenny wanted to stay at home with her new family.

After graduating with honors, Jenny began her teaching career but spent all her spare time looking for her lost family.

# Chapter 17

Jenny and Cal dated for six months before Cal proposed. After a small, intimate wedding with family and close friends, Jenny and Cal took off on their honeymoon to Cabo.

While they were walking on the beach one evening, their conversation turned to Jenny's parents. "Cal, for years I worried that my parents would look for me. Shelter life wasn't good, but the thought of going back to them was terrifying. Were they just glad to be rid of us? Did they stay in that house next door? Did they stay together?"

She had never asked these questions before, but now that she had married into a family that had so much money, she was afraid her parents might get wind of it and cause trouble.

Cal stopped abruptly. With a look of disbelief, he asked, "Are you serious? Don't you know what happened to your parents?"

"No! And why are you so shocked that I would have misgivings about them ever finding me?"

"Oh my God, Jenny, I can't believe you don't know. It was headline news for days!"

"What news?" Jenny asked in a trembling voice. "After the night we were taken away, I was in a daze for months, like a zombie."

Cal pulled her close to him, wrapping her in his arms. Realizing she was loved and safe, Jenny apologized for being such a baby. They sat down on the moonlit beach and Cal filled her in on what he remembered about that night.

"I know it's hard to believe when you think of the rotten kid I used to be. When I answered your knock at the door, I was ready to make a smart aleck remark, as usual. But when I saw your face, I forgot all that. I had never before seen such pain and dread in anyone's eyes. I knew you were in some kind of terrible trouble. I know I've told you this before, but you changed my life.

"And after the police took you and the other kids away, everyone in my family felt awful. We didn't admit it at first, but we knew you and your family were lost. Dad remarked that he was glad it was over, and Mom kept repeating there was nothing they could do. But in their hearts they both knew a good meal and a warm bed would have been in order.

"I escaped to my room, but I couldn't sleep, so I finally went into the living room, where my parents were watching TV. Nobody wanted to talk, but we didn't want to be alone with our own thoughts either. About fifteen minutes later, we smelled smoke. Dad ran outside to see where it was coming from and then rushed back inside and screamed at my mom to call 911. The Farrow house was ablaze.

"We all ran into the street, afraid the fire would spread to our house. By the time the fire trucks arrived, it was eating at your parents' roof. Eventually the roof caved in, and the house was lost.

"We found out later that your mom's friend, Angel, went right home after telling you to come over here. She didn't want to get in the middle of any trouble between your parents. But when she got home, she blurted out the story to her husband, telling him that Mike was not the father of Sheila's new baby.

"Her husband thought her story sounded suspicious and wanted to know how she knew all this. She claimed that Sheila had told her she was afraid because the baby's real father had green eyes and so did the baby. She didn't know what Mike would do to her when he realized the baby wasn't his.

"Angel's husband went out looking for your dad. The two were bar buddies, and he knew he would find Mike at Patsy's Tavern down the street. When he found Mike, he told him there was trouble at home and that the kids had run away.

"He should have left it at that but he didn't. He also informed Mike that the baby wasn't his. At first Mike called him a liar, even though he really didn't trust Sheila. He demanded to know where the information came from. After hearing Angel's story, Mike threw a full glass of beer at Angel's husband and stormed out of the bar.

"No one knows exactly what went on inside that house when Mike got home, but the firemen found two dead bodies when they got there."

Shocked and yet at the same time relieved, Jenny just whispered, "All this time I've been afraid of a couple of ghosts."

One year later Jenny delivered a beautiful baby boy. His eyes were not green, but his name was Craig.

# LILY

# Chapter 18

Lily returned to Drayton House after a few days in the hospital. Her concussion hadn't been serious and the gash in her head was beginning to heal.

When Ben picked up the little girl from the hospital, he asked the doctor if she would follow up and request that Drayton remove the word *unadoptable* from Lily's file. He hoped the suggestion would have more weight coming from a professional.

Marie empathized with this little girl whose situation so paralleled her own, but in two days she was leaving for a second stint with Doctors Without Borders and would be away for at least three months. She promised to do all she could to help the child as soon as she got back, but for now nothing could be done.

As Ben fastened her seat belt, Lily sobbed and begged him not to take her back to Drayton. He tried to calm her down by telling her they were going for a little surprise first.

A few minutes later, Ben pulled up to his favorite diner. Lily perked up as soon as she saw the shiny silver building. "What a pretty house. What's inside?" she wanted to know.

"It's called a diner, Lily. It's a place where you eat delicious food."

The waitress noticed the tear stains on Lily's face as soon as the little girl walked in. "Well, well, haven't seen you in a while, Ben. Who's your new friend?"

"Good morning, Jan! This is Lily."

Turning to Lily, Ben asked her if there was something she really wanted. When she replied that she only liked his soup, Ben decided to order a few tempting things from the menu. He told Jan to bring them scrambled eggs and toast, a hamburger, and chicken noodle soup, hoping there were be something in that mini-buffet that would please Lily. And he ordered an egg, cheese, and bacon bagel for himself.

Lily was a poor eater, and given the unappetizing food she was used to at Drayton, she wasn't in any rush to eat. The fact that she was sitting in this shiny castle with Ben temporarily eased her dread of returning to the shelter.

Jan had no idea who this child was, and she hesitated to question Ben. She didn't know much about him and had no idea if he was married or had grandchildren or even where he lived. He was just a nice guy who loved diner food. But after one look at the little girl, Jan decided she was going to bring a smile to that sad little face. She fixed up a sampler platter of a mini-hamburger with a few French fries, a little ramekin with scrambled eggs, toast, and a small bowl of chicken soup. She also included a glass of apple juice.

All this special preparation took extra time, and meanwhile completed orders were backing up on the service table. The chef glared at Jan. Customers wanted to know where their food was. But Jan just wanted to see a smile as she placed Lily's special platter in front of her.

Lily, whose normal voice was soft and barely audible, squealed with sheer pleasure, "That looks so yummy! Thank you so much. I never saw anything so good!"

Everyone in that diner smiled at Lily's excitement, and her simple words of gratitude surprised and touched them. After a few moments, people started to applaud as they strained to get a better glimpse of Lily.

After Jan told Lily she was more than welcome, she went back to the kitchen with tears rolling down her cheeks. The little girl was dressed in drab, hand-me-down, washed-out clothes—certainly not an outfit a mother, father, or grandfather would choose for an outing. And it was amazing how grateful she was for something that most other kids her age would take for granted. Jan just couldn't figure out the connection between this waif-like child and the well-groomed Ben.

Jan rushed to serve the backorders, at first not noticing the change that had occurred in the diner. Impatient customers were suddenly chattering happily and sipping on orange juice or coffee while they waited for their food to be served. There were no more complaints about delays; and when their meals arrived, the customers dug in with gusto, as if they were tasting bacon and eggs for the very first time.

Meanwhile, Lily enjoyed her sampler, expressing glee with every bite, though her tiny stomach filled quickly. As customers finished their meals and left the diner, they stopped to have a chat with the exuberant little girl. Lily invited each one to take a taste of her wonderful treat.

That day a small child inspired the people she met to appreciate the simple things in life a bit more.

When the chef called Jan into the kitchen, she was nervous; but she was pleasantly surprised when he said he'd like to meet the child who was responsible for the change in the customers.

He shook Lily's hand and told her his name was Sam. When he asked if she would like to see where the food was cooked, Lily nodded and soon found herself riding on the big man's shoulders as he navigated around tables and patrons to get to the kitchen.

Lily's eyes were wide with awe as she watched the cooks frying eggs and sausages and flipping pancakes into the air. Because the cooks had an audience, the pancakes reached new heights and not a one missed the pan when it came back down.

When Ben asked for the bill, Sam, who was also the owner, smiled as he told him there was no bill. "We should pay *you* for all the happy customers that sweet girl generated."

As Lily walked out the door, Sam handed her a bag of cookies and told her to come back for another visit soon.

As Ben strapped Lily into her seat, he asked, "Did you like your surprise, Pretty Flower?"

"Oh yes, Ben, I really and truly loved it!" the little girl exclaimed.

Arriving at the shelter, Ben lifted Lily out of the van and hugged her as he put her down on the sidewalk. "You're the best girl anywhere," he whispered in her ear.

Those words stayed with her as she slowly walked into the dingy rooms smelling of disinfectant. She was back at Drayton House—her home.

# Chapter 19

Ben sat in his van for several minutes remembering another unadoptable resident who had lived at the shelter years before. Marie's life in the shelter had followed the same path as Lily's. She had suffered hellish treatment at the hands of child predators, both at the shelter and at private foster homes.

That survivor was now grown up. Dr. Marie Eagan was a respected medical doctor whose compassion had earned her the nickname "Mother Theresa" among her patients and their families, while her role as director of first-year interns inspired them to call her "Boss Lady."

Ben knew that the past haunted Marie. He had been a much younger man when she was at the shelter, and when she told him about the abuse there he thought he was doing the right thing in reporting the problem to the manager. But as it turned out, he had reported the problem to the wrong person, and Ben had never forgiven himself for not taking a more active role in protecting her.

After the scandals came to light, improvements were made at Drayton, and stricter employee background searches were ordered by the state. However, tight funding limited the salaries offered. Applicants who should never be allowed to work with children were hired and entrusted with the well-being of the wards of the state.

Managers like Mrs. Andrews possessed the minimal qualifications for their job description. She focused on only the most obvious day-to-day tasks that needed her attention. She avoided any situations that might require an advocate.

It wasn't that she was corrupt, but she had no desire to get involved with the emotional side of running the shelter. She ran Drayton strictly as a business, ignoring the fact that the top priority of a shelter should be to provide a safe, receptive, and welcoming environment for abused or abandoned children.

Ben and Rose Romero were the only two employees at Drayton who had deep concerns about the development of children spending their childhood in an institution where impersonal caretakers replaced parental love.

Rose's qualifications for her position as Shelter Coordinator were impeccable, but her heavy caseload impeded her ability to deal effectively with the complex cases she was assigned. No case was ever simple. Each one required investigations and suggested solutions, and that took time.

Twice a month Rose checked into any of the children's complaints. But since most of the children assigned to Drayton remained there less than three months, only immediate problems could be addressed.

Because Lily was a long-term resident as well as a compliant child, there wasn't much time left for her. She needed love and attention, and fifteen minutes twice a month didn't cut it. But Rose adored Lily and was impressed by her advanced capabilities, so whenever she could find some extra time, Rose devised educational development plans for Lily. The staff was supposed to implement the lessons. While they were certainly capable of working with a four-year-old, their excuses for not handling the plans amazed Rose.

Even Mrs. Andrews claimed she had no time to spend with Lily. It would only take a half hour a day, but she had no time. The house manager found time to watch her favorite daytime soap as well as take a two-hour lunch break every day, but she had no time for Lily. Rose seethed at the irresponsibility of the Drayton staff. When she shared her disapproval with Ben, he suggested she leave Lily's plans with him.

Every morning from June to September, Ben spread a long table outside with items that he knew the children would enjoy, such as Legos, building blocks, puzzles, paints, coloring books, and storybooks. Drinks and healthy snacks were laid out on a smaller table. The children pulled up chairs to the long table and spent a few hours doing their favorite activities. Just before they went back to the main house for lunch, Ben would read aloud a few chapters from a children's classic.

Many of the children were so emotionally scarred that they lacked the desire or ability to sit at that table. Some found it difficult to concentrate, and there was often friction caused by the unruly kids. This could easily prove frustrating for many an adult, but Ben's patience, understanding, and personal dedication won over even the most reluctant child. Lily flourished.

Ben's setup was ideal for the staff members. Anything that lessened their responsibilities and gave them some break time was a bonus.

As cooler weather approached, Mrs. Andrews offered Ben an unused room to continue his sessions inside. Children who only spent a few days in the shelter usually didn't attend school, so this gave them some mental stimulation and provided an opportunity for some fun.

Ben loved spending this time with the kids, but he never neglected his main responsibility, which was maintaining the property. In addition to making or contracting out any necessary repairs to the building, he also enhanced the grounds. He planted a variety of flowers to brighten the dreary areas and designed a vegetable garden to provide some fresh produce that the cook could use to make healthier meals.

Daytime for Lily went well if Ben was in sight. The two of them also managed to make a stop at the diner at least once a week. If Lily had been bullied or picked on by the older children, Ben tried to work in a trip to the duck pond or an extra diner visit.

The other shelter kids didn't know about the duck pond or the diner, but Ben did take time each day to do something with each child. Most, with the exception of Lily, were there for a short time and would either go back home soon or enter the long-term foster care system. Some would even be adopted. Only Lily's case file had been stamped "unadoptable."

So the duck pond and the diner were Lily and Ben's secret. Mrs. Andrews was the only other person at the shelter who knew about their little adventures. As long as Ben didn't ask her for any money to fund these excursions, they had her OK.

Jan looked forward to the twosome's drop-ins at the diner. As soon as Ben opened the door, Lily rushed in to hug the staff. Sam and Jan would usually receive a picture drawn especially for them. A special spot right near the entrance was set aside for Lily's drawings. Jan took time to arrange the illustrations on the bulletin board on the wall. A talented busboy created the heading "LILY'S WORKS OF ART" in bold embellished letters.

The regular patrons made it their first stop to admire the drawings before being seated. The pictures were surprisingly well developed for a four year old. Her ideas were clearly expressed. Most were happy scenes depicting the duck pond, Ben's vegetable garden, Sam flipping pancakes, or Jan serving customers at the tables. But every once in a while her drawing included a small crying child wearing a shabby dress like Lily often wore.

It wasn't long before Lily's pictures came to the attention of a local newspaper and a reporter came in to interview Ben, Lily, Jan, and Sam. When his article appeared in the newspaper, Lily's background and any mention of Drayton House were omitted. Ben had been adamant about that. The article created so much interest in the diner that Sam couldn't keep up with his newfound customers, so he added more staff.

Sam and Jan always took time to sit with Lily and Ben when they were there. Lily was so comfortable with her new friends that her conversations often drew attention to incidents that concerned Ben.

# Chapter 20

After one visit to the diner during which Lily had mentioned the shelter and the boy who had bullied her there, Ben decided he owed Jan and Sam an explanation. One afternoon while in town to purchase some pipes to repair the plumbing at Drayton, Ben stopped at the diner around 2:30, knowing there would be fewer customers at that time.

Jan and Sam had already come to the conclusion that Lily's life was unhappy, but now Ben went into detail as he described Lily's situation. He also talked about himself and his role at Drayton, revealing his widower status and his life in the small cottage on the grounds.

Ben did not want them to think of him as a pauper, so he explained that he stayed at the shelter to do what he could for displaced children. Living in the cottage cost little. He put aside money to assist when he could. What he didn't mention were the financial contributions he had made to Marie's education that had helped her become a doctor. He had paid for her books, her share of her rent, and other necessities that came up during her years in college and then medical school. And his encouragement kept her going when she became discouraged by the obstacles she had to overcome along the way.

As soon as she began practicing medicine, Marie devised a plan to pay him back. Ben didn't want to hear anything about it until Marie came up with an idea that he use the money she repaid him to help another shelter child. Ben liked that idea, and so he finally acquiesced.

As Ben related his story, Jan's admiration for him grew. He was the direct opposite of her former husband. After years of mentally abusing her and losing one job after another, he ran off with a woman of similar character, never to be seen again. She was glad he was gone, but he had also left with her car and every bit of the small savings they had put away.

Fortunately, Sam heard about her problems. He was about to trade in his car for a new one, but instead he offered her the vehicle. He and his wife also owned a carriage house that they offered her as a temporary home.

The situation worked out so well that Jan stayed on for years. The couple asked a nominal rent, which enabled Jan to put money aside. The three became as close as a family. Jan was finally free and happy after an oppressive marriage and her life flowed smoothly, although she did long for companionship similar to the closeness the couple enjoyed.

A few weeks after Ben had told her about Lily and himself, Jan invited him to dinner at her home. Ben was taken by surprise, as he really had not socialized since his wife's death. His one love had been taken away from him far too early, so he contented himself by trying to brighten the dismal life of the shelter children, even if they were only there for a day.

The thought of spending an evening with Jan was very appealing, as he had really enjoyed the diner conversations they had been having, so he warmly accepted her invitation. Jan asked if Lily could join them. Ben's eyes clouded as he explained the ridiculous rule that excluded him from taking Lily into his home for the night or even out for an evening because he lived alone.

Over the years, Ben had offered to take several children to stay at the cottage, but even though anyone associated with Ben knew he had integrity beyond reproach, the answer was always no. Instead the children were dumped into often unloving homes, and they had to be placed in these temporary homes by 6 p.m.

Jan was delighted with the prospect of spending time with this unselfish, gentle man who seemed to be so unappreciated by the shelter, and she enjoyed planning a special roast beef dinner for him. As Ben enjoyed the home-cooked meal, he listened attentively as Jan revealed a bit about herself. She didn't want to bore him with the details of her failed marriage, so she steered the conversation to other things like recent movies. She also mentioned Sam's plans to expand the diner to accommodate the increase in business.

Ben felt the comfort that enjoying another's company brings. He slowly divulged the void the loss of his wife had left. Not wanting to sound maudlin, he too changed the subject to compliment Jan on her delicious meal.

The topic then turned to Drayton. Although many stories were left untold, Jan heard enough to know that dark and cruel incidents took place there and that many young innocents suffered. Ben mentioned that some improvements had finally been made after a scandal. Children were no longer exposed to sexual predators, and many new rules were implemented. For example, two staffers were required to assist children preparing for bed; in fact, children were never to be alone with only one staff member. But although there were many new rules, none of them addressed a child's need for a loving, nurturing environment.

# Chapter 21

Several months went by. Night placements were still unhappy times for Lily, but her general situation was so much happier now that she could look forward to her visits at the diner. Jan and Ben's relationship quickly went from friendly companionship to wedding plans. Both of them felt they had wasted too many years alone.

One afternoon as Jan completed her preliminary packing in preparation for the big move to Ben's place, she thought about how much she loved his cottage. The care Ben took to create an inviting and comfortable home was something she had never experienced. Her parents had separated when she was in high school, after years of turmoil, and neither of them had ever taken any interest in creating a welcoming home.

Soon Ben would pick her up and load her car as well as his own. They would drive to Ben's cottage, and Jan would stay there to unpack before they went back to her place for the next load. And that evening she would finally have the chance to meet Dr. Marie Eagan, who was like a daughter to Ben.

Just that morning Ben had received a call from Marie. She had recently returned from her tour to the Middle East with Doctors Without Borders. She was safe, close by, and happy, and she briefly mentioned that she was deeply in love. There was so much news to share that Ben suggested she and her boyfriend join him and Jan for a celebration dinner. Ben gave Marie the address of a restaurant where they would meet at 7 p.m.

While Jan unpacked, Ben went to pick up Lily and drop her off for her overnight with still another family. Lily was waiting in the office with her usual somber and serious expression, which always saddened Ben.

As Ben walked in, Mrs. Andrews looked up from the telephone. Angry and frustrated, she complained that she had called every family on her list without any luck. No one was able to take Lily that night. Every other child was already assigned and Mike, the other driver, had dropped them off and then left for the evening. To complicate matters, the only aide who worked at Drayton overnight had called in sick, and Mrs. Andrews had her own plans that she was not willing to cancel.

After asking Mrs. Andrews if they could move to another room so that Lily couldn't hear their conversation, Ben asked once again if he could take Lily for the evening, assuring her that Jan would be with him.

"Ben, how many times have I told you that only vetted homes are eligible? Now that you will be married, you and Jan will be able to apply, but that doesn't help tonight. I do still have names from last year's list and I guess I'll just have to start calling them."

After five more calls to families on her old list, she finally received a positive response. She was so excited to find someone willing to take Lily that she forgot to question why the family had not updated their information. Ben noted the house was farther away than all of the other families they used. He would definitely run into traffic, which would make it difficult to make the restaurant reservation. He thought about asking Mike to come back to drop Lily off, but he didn't want to upset Lily even more by switching drivers on her.

Ben called Jan and asked her to meet him at the restaurant, explaining that he might be a little late. Then he loaded an unhappy child into the van. As he drove Lily to the new family, he told her all about the wedding plans that he and Jan were making and assured her that soon she would be able to spend the nights with them.

That news excited Lily. She clapped her hands and began joyfully singing her repertoire of songs. Good things really did happen to deserving people!

# Chapter 22

The Drayton van pulled up to a large white house surrounded by neatly trimmed shrubs, a manicured lawn, and a cluster of golden yellow daylilies. Ben also noticed a swing set in the backyard. The welcoming house encouraged Ben to hope that these were caring people. A middle-aged petite woman answered the door. She was wearing an apron, which was always a good sign.

As Lily put down her battered suitcase in the entryway, Ben announced that she, Jan, and he were going to have a breakfast party at the diner in the morning. Lily was full of smiles as he left.

Looking at his watch, Ben realized he would be fine with the time. As he pulled out of the driveway, he glanced at the house one more time. Something bothered him, but he couldn't figure out exactly what it was. As he drove toward the restaurant, his gut feeling told him to go back and take Lily away from the big white house. But he ignored the warning.

Once he saw Jan's car in the parking lot, anticipated pleasure overtook his doubts. She was wearing a soft pink chiffon dress adorned with the white rose corsage he had had delivered that afternoon.

Meanwhile, Mrs. Andrews sat at her desk preparing to leave for the evening. The building took on an almost sinister aura when one was there alone. Finally she got up and put the old list back in the folder labeled "Eligible Temporary Shelter Residences." The folder was heavy. It needed cleaning up, as there were probably outdated items that should be removed.

As she filed the folder, a smaller envelope fell out. It had never been opened, but the postmark sent a shock wave through her as she realized it was an update from months ago. It was from the state and listed all the ineligible families and pertinent information. Her first overwhelming concern was a frightening possibility that children were being sent to homes that were removed from the list. This list was not made up of families who didn't want to participate but ones who were removed from the list as unsuitable, with documented reasons included.

Mrs. Andrews planned to shorten her dinner plans with her daughter and family so that she could review the folder, just to be on the safe side. Once home, she would check the updates for any names from last year's list. She had used that old list multiple times, and she knew the state would not forgive an oversight like that. Occasionally the removal of a family was voluntary, but most of the deletions were a result of serious infractions.

When dinner was finished, she used a headache as an excuse and apologized as she made her exit. As soon as she got home, she opened the envelop somewhat apprehensively, spreading out the old and new lists of assigned homes on her kitchen table. Attached to each formal dismissal were a newspaper clipping, evidence of criminal records, and any other evidence documenting that household's removal from the list.

There were twenty removals. The manager checked the list against her old list, skimming quickly until house number seven jumped out. Two weeks ago one of the shelter children had spent the night there. Her fingers shook just lifting the page to see the evidence for removal. The first paragraph calmed her down. The woman of the household had received two DUI citations, reason enough for dismissal but not necessarily indicating endangerment to an overnight guest.

Mrs. Andrews continued to cross-check the lists. Number seventeen had also been removed from the approved list. Feeling a sudden tightening in her chest, she forced herself to go to today's schedule. One child had been placed in that household. Her worst fears were realized when she read the evidence attached to the file.

The husband had been indicted for the long-term sexual abuse of an eleven-year-old girl who was a foster child. However, the judge was forced to dismiss the case when the girl testified that she had lied. A news photo showed the girl being embraced by her foster parents with the caption "FORGIVENESS."

# Chapter 23

Even though the man was exonerated, the state immediately removed this family's certification. Yet right now poor little Lily was in that man's clutches, and Mrs. Andrews was responsible. A surge of guilt coupled with fear engulfed the shelter manager, who had always prided herself that she ran a tight and efficient business. She felt sickened at the thought of Lily in the hands of such a predator.

Mrs. Andrews looked at her watch, noting that three hours had transpired since Lily had been dropped off. Unaware of Ben and Jan's celebration, she quickly called Ben's landline, which rang and then went to voicemail. The same thing happened when she called his cell, but this time she left a message.

"Ben, this is Angela. Please call me as soon as you get this message. It's very important."

She grabbed her jacket and purse, ran to her car, and drove straight to the address of the big white house.

# Chapter 24

At the restaurant Ben ordered a bottle of champagne, which was quite out of character for him. It wasn't that he was frugal, but there hadn't been any special occasions like this over the past several years.

The evening couldn't have been more perfect. The two couples enjoyed the fine food, the convivial atmosphere, and each other's company. They had lingered over coffee to extend the special evening. While they were waiting for the check, Jan asked if Lily was excited about breakfast in the morning. Ben said the little girl had been full of smiles when she heard about the surprise.

At 10 p.m. they said good-night and walked slowly to their respective cars. Ben mentioned to Jan that he didn't have a good feeling about leaving Lily, even though the house looked very cozy and a pleasant woman had answered the door.

He paused a moment, then continued to tell Jan that he wished he had gone in with Lily, something he usually did when he was concerned. But he was worried about getting to the restaurant on time. He suddenly remembered that he had also turned his cell phone off when he got to the restaurant and wondered why he hadn't just switched it to vibrate while he was inside. Now he quickly reached for his phone and turned it on, noticing the missed voicemail.

At first he couldn't figure out who Angela was. Then it dawned on him. Mrs. Andrews had never referred to herself as Angela to anyone at the shelter. She also never called him after hours. Bolts of alarm shot through his entire body. There was also another call, but he didn't take time to check the message. If he had, he would have been even more terrified.

Ben immediately called Mrs. Andrews, but there was no answer. Once again he felt the seizing in his gut and he knew that Lily was in danger. Suddenly in a hurry, he and Jan rushed to his car, leaving her car in the restaurant's lot.

The trip to the white house seemed endless. Jan turned on soft music and pointed out the possibility that Mrs. Andrews' call could be about something else entirely. But deep down they both knew it was about Lily.

As they approached the cul-de-sac where the white house was located, they heard sirens behind them. Pulling over to let an ambulance by, Ben panicked. As he got closer, he saw several police cars and another ambulance outside the house where he had dropped Lily off. Weaving between the vehicles, Ben screamed, "Why oh why did I leave you, my precious Lily Flower?"

Ben scraped the curb as he stopped the car and jumped out. One ambulance stood in front of the house as paramedics loaded someone inside and then quickly shut the door. Ben had no idea of the age or the sex of the victim, but he thought it looked too large to be a child.

The police stopped Ben before he reached the manicured walk that led to the wide open front door. He screamed over and over that his little girl was inside. His plaintiff wail reached the ears of the chief of police, who was just coming out of the house.

By this time, Jan had caught up to Ben and Angela had also arrived. The police chief pulled them aside, somberly relating the sad details to them.

# Chapter 25

The aproned lady led Lily up two flights of stairs to the top floor of the house. She did not offer to carry the four year old's suitcase, even though Lily was struggling. When they finally got to a small room at the top, the exhausted child noticed the lady's smile had been replaced by a scowl.

After telling Lily to be downstairs for dinner at 6:00, she closed the door, never thinking about how a four year old was supposed to find a clock in an unfamiliar house or even wondering if the child knew how to tell time. It didn't seem to dawn on her that children can be frightened when left alone in unfamiliar surroundings. As the lady descended the stairs again, Lily heard her shout to someone named Carla that dinner was at 6:00.

Lily was able to wing it more than most of her peers. Telling time was no problem if she could find a clock, but not knowing the location of the bathroom upset her.

Pushing down on the door handle, Lily left her room, only to discover that the immediate world beyond her room was far from inviting. A narrow hall ran the length of the house, with doors on either side.

It was necessary for Lily to open two doors before she found the bathroom. As soon as she got back into the hall, a muffled cry caught her attention. Following the sound, she knocked at the door where the moaning came from, assuming the crying came from someone named Carla

"Carla, what's the matter?" Lily whispered softly.

Carla was shocked to hear her name called so sweetly. She didn't think it could be another foster child. After that court incident Carla surmised they were no longer eligible to be foster parents. Why they took in a child overnight amazed her. They didn't need the money.

"Go away," Carla hissed back.

Lily found her way back to her room and stared at the clock until the hands told her it was time to go downstairs. When she left her room again, there was no sign of Carla. As she got down to the second floor, Lily noticed a wide hall revealing several open doors. One was close enough for Lily to see a big bed inside. She wondered why the woman had put her and Carla in that dusty, dreary area upstairs when there were lots of nice bedrooms down here.

Reaching the large foyer at the bottom of the steps, Lily spotted the dining room. Two people were sitting there, but neither of them spoke. No one even told her where to sit. A place was set beside the girl Lily assumed was Carla, so she sat down there.

Lily had never seen dishes and glasses in such beautiful colors. The gleaming silverware and table cloth with matching napkins amazed her too.

The lady, still wearing her apron, brought in dishes of food that smelled delicious. The man sliced the meat, took two huge slices, and then placed the platter in the middle of the table.

The woman came over to Lily and fixed her a plate with a selection of delectable food. She did the same thing with Carla. No one even picked up a fork until the man lifted his. At the side of his plate was a glass with something that wasn't water but had a particular smell. He emptied his glass with the same speed as he stuffed food into his mouth, and Lily noticed that the glass was refilled several times.

Lily took a small portion of each item placed on her plate. It was all so good. She broke the silence by declaring how good the dinner was. The woman nodded her head in response.

As the man continued drinking, his demeanor changed from stern, proper, and silent to slipshod, loud, and insolent. Lily had a small appetite. Though she took her time, she was finished quickly. She eyed Carla's plate throughout the meal, noticing that little food disappeared. Carla just moved food around with one hand while she held her head up with the other.

Lily had seen many children at the shelter who wept in agony. This girl's torment seemed beyond grief. The only thing she finished was her roll. Lily wanted to help her, so instead of taking the roll from the small plate that was next to her dinner plate for herself, she wrapped her roll in her napkin, got up, and placed the roll on Carla's plate, being careful not to let her fingers touch the roll. That was the way they did it at the shelter.

Carla saw it as the only act of kindness she had received in years. Her moaning switched to heartbreaking sobs. Lily had no idea what she had done to cause this.

"I wanted to give you the roll to make you happy. Don't cry."

The sobs increased. The man rose unsteadily from his chair; the liquor had found its mark. Pointing his finger at Lily, he shrieked a few drunken expletives. The words meant nothing to her, but his voice petrified her.

"You little brat, look what you've done. Go the hell back to your room before I beat the crap out of you!"

Then he turned to Carla. "Bitch, stop the goddam crying. Get up to your room and get out of my sight."

Then this disgusting form of humanity sat down, filled his plate, and shoveled the food down as if the outbreak had never occurred.

# Chapter 26

Carla was ahead of Lily climbing those abominable steps. Lily tripped and fell down several steps, scraping her leg. Carla heard her stumble. At first she was just going to get to her room as fast as possible, but Lily awakened something in her that had been dormant for years. She changed directions and scooped up Lily, taking her back to her room and pushing a chair under the door knob.

Carla brought out a box hidden in the back of her tiny closet. She pulled out a doll wearing a skating outfit. Another smaller box contained several more outfits.

"You can play with these while you're here. It's still early, and that bastard won't come up for hours."

Lily knew this was a bad place to be. She told Carla she didn't like the man and woman and asked if they were bad people. Carla told her they were the worst people in the world.

The mistreated girl felt the need to relate all the abuses she had suffered from these people for the last three years. She also described the repeated rapes she had endured. Lily didn't understand the details, but she did know that what the man had done caused Carla pain.

Lily told Carla she should run away and tell the police what happened. Carla's answer was even more frightening. She did try once but the husband, Bernard, got her away from the people who were supposed to be protecting her. He only had a few minutes with her, but that was enough time to tell her he would kill her if she didn't tell the authorities that she had lied. She was so afraid that she did as he demanded, and they sent her back home with him.

Carla told Lily she also suspected that Bernard used to take pictures of naked little children but had stopped after that incident. No other kids had been to the house since then—until Lily.

This information overwhelmed and frightened Lily. "I'm going to call my friend Ben. He'll know what to do," she told Carla. "He gave me his number. I have it in my suitcase. Do you have a phone?"

Carla shook her head while throwing up her hands. There were probably landlines in the second floor bedrooms. Carla never tried to find one because there was no one to call.

Lily only wanted to get away from that place. She waited on the steps for a few minutes, hoping neither of those bad people were on the second floor. She moved swiftly to the first room, the one with the big bed. A telephone rested on the night table. Lily took the phone off its cradle and took it upstairs to Carla's room.

Carla told her to call from her own room, as it would be safer there if Bernard should come upstairs. Lily took the number from her suitcase. It was very hard to push the correct numbers. It took a while for those little fingers to accomplish the task. The sound of the phone ringing gave her hope that she could leave this horrible place.

As soon as she heard Ben's voice, she tried to talk to him, but then she just heard a buzz. Lily ran into Carla's room whimpering that Ben wouldn't talk to her.

Carla dialed the number and realized the call was going into voicemail. She gave Lily the phone, telling her to have Ben come right to the house as soon as he got the message.

Carla realized the phone had to be put back. She slipped down the stairs, put the phone on the cradle, and dashed back upstairs. Lily had to be protected, so she took the little girl to her room, telling her to keep her clothes on. She gave Lily the doll to sleep with, then closed her door.

Somehow Lily managed to fall asleep but was awakened awhile later by voices in the hall. Lily opened her door enough to see Carla and Bernard struggling, and his hand was over her mouth.

"You little bitch, shut up. You know I'll kill you if you make noise," Bernard uttered as he dragged Carla into her room and toward the bed.

As frightened as she was, Lily ran to help Carla. Bernard was about to lock the door when Lily pushed it open, hitting him with her small fists. At that moment Bernard realized he was through. Somebody would pick her up in the morning and she would tell everything she had seen. All would be over for him.

While he was trying to think what to do, he heard his wife calling, wondering what was going on. Carla managed to bite the hand he was still holding over her mouth. She screamed as loud as she could. Up until now she had feared for her own life, but suddenly she realized there was something more important. By sharing her roll, that little girl had broken down the icy wall that had been holding in Carla's emotions. Now she was determined to protect Lily, no matter what it took.

Carla wrenched herself free from Bernard's grip, trying to grab Lily and make a run for it. Bernard was too strong for her, though. He pushed her back toward a large standing mirror. Her head hit it squarely with such force that the mirror shattered into many pieces-- some large, some minute, but all deadly. A large pointed dagger slashed Carla's shoulder, causing her to bleed profusely.

Still conscious but in excruciating pain, Carla reached for another huge piece of mirror with a sharp edge. She picked up the shard of glass and slowly managed to stand up, even though she felt dizzy.

Bernard's back was to Carla. He was about to pick up Lily, who was also screaming for help. He had to get rid of her. With all the strength she could muster, Carla aimed that dagger right between his shoulders. The weapon hit its mark, and Bernard slumped over.

By now, Bernard's wife had reached the top of the steps. Rushing into the room, she saw Carla cowering in a corner while her husband lay bleeding on the floor. Lily was standing by the door, frozen with fear. The crazed woman screamed at Carla, who didn't respond. She was drifting between light and dark, yet wanting with all her heart to see Lily safely away from this horror.

Bernard's wife looked at Lily and made a quick decision. If Lily were dead, she could say Carla had killed her. Carla looked close to death herself; and if she died, no one could dispute this story. Then she and Bernard would be fine. She picked up another large piece of mirror and turned toward the terrified child.

# MARIE

# Chapter 27

Ben looked at the final box that was part of the move separating his old life from the new. This change was not the one he and Laura had planned but one that circumstances orchestrated. If fate had allowed their original plan to be carried out, he and Laura, his wife of thirty years, would be at their Morrison Avenue home, raking leaves and exchanging summer clothes for winter while making plans for Thanksgiving.

After years of trying, they found themselves childless. That was a disappointment as the two were such caring individuals. They certainly had all the good-parenting essentials. And so temporary foster children from a nearby shelter were often guests in their house. They used the money the state paid for foster care to buy the children presents they would never receive at the shelter.

Ben had joined the police force the year before he married Laura and had advanced from a rookie to the position of managing the detective squad. Ben's professional life could certainly have led to cynicism since he was well acquainted with the depraved side of humanity. Instead, he was known as a dedicated officer as well as a stickler for following a case without bias or malice.

Ben and Laura had shared a life of a cohesive love, deep respect, and a mutual code of ethical priorities. But then within just one year the serenity of a productive, happy life together spiraled downward. Laura was diagnosed with pancreatic cancer. She struggled for six months but gave up the fight when life lost its quality. Ben's enthusiasm for life dissipated to a mere trickle the moment Laura took her last breath.

Proof of the high regard Ben had earned throughout his career in law enforcement was the funeral attendance for Laura. He was grateful for the kindness shown by his friends and co-workers, but unfortunately their caring did little to fill the empty void left by Laura's death.

Some feel their career is a salvation in a time of sorrow. With Ben, the passion ceased to exist. He became concerned that his productivity would be affected. After thirty years on the force, he turned in his badge.

Money was not an issue, as Ben would have an excellent pension. And Laura had inherited a hefty inheritance from her parents that she and Ben had never touched. Now all of it was his.

Concerned friends cautioned him to wait before addressing any more major decisions. He gave that credence, as he had no future plan. And so he spent some time beginning to consider and then cross off options. Travel without Laura was not appealing. She had been the organizer of all their vacations. She was the one who made them work.

As the months wore on, the house was no longer the place of comfort it once was. Memories of Laura permeated every room. At times memories bring warm messages from the past. But for Ben, more often they just emphasized his tremendous loss.

Within six months, Ben made the decision to sell the house. Even though he and Laura had no relatives, they had numerous friends, so he didn't want to start over in an unfamiliar setting. But nothing appealed to him when it came to living quarters. Ben knew he wanted something smaller, but he just wasn't satisfied with anything he saw.

One evening while trying to get interested in a television program, he realized that finding a new place to live wasn't the issue. The real problem was that he did not know what he wanted to do for the rest of his life.

A few days later he received a call from his friend Dale, asking him over for dinner. Ben usually avoided these invitations, feeling that people were just feeling sorry for him. However, Dale and his wife, Marge, were a pleasant couple, so Ben looked forward to being their guest.

As expected, the evening never lacked for conversation. Dale, who was an accountant, mentioned Drayton House at one point. Ben was already familiar with the shelter but didn't know that it was under new management. Dale told him that the place was run down and getting worse since they had no funds for regular maintenance. Marge mentioned she was going there the next day to deliver some children's clothes.

Ben had some toys Laura had stored for future visits from the shelter children. He had forgotten about them until this conversation, but now he asked Marge if he could go with her and donate the toys.

# Chapter 28

A short, wiry, unsmiling man greeted Marge and Ben when they arrived at Drayton the next day. He was preoccupied with a tour he was about to start. A group from the Health Department was there to make a preliminary inspection. Mr. Sourpuss introduced himself as Lou Harden, the manager of Drayton House. After a few minutes he asked if they would like to join the tour.

Ben's eyes surveyed the walks and paths throughout the large piece of property. As they conducted their inspection, one of the group members tripped on a broken piece of cement. Her look conveyed disgust at Drayton's condition. She could not contain her annoyance as she pointed out the hazards that children could easily encounter.

Mr. Harden quickly mentioned that a top priority was the hiring of a maintenance/gardener/handyman, adding there was even the cottage to be offered at a nominal rent if that were of interest. Ben lagged behind, making mental notes of what was required to make this place more appealing, especially for the children.

This was Ben's bailiwick. He did almost every bit of repair in his home, and his yard was the pride of the entire neighborhood. There was a vegetable garden that fed the neighborhood in the summer. A flower garden strictly for children had small benches so they could sit and observe butterflies and bumblebees at work. Children responded with gentle enthusiasm. Whenever Laura noticed children sitting there, she brought out cookies and lemonade, as well as age-appropriate books. Sometimes she would add crayons and coloring books. During the summer, the place to be for young children was Ben's Children's Garden.

As they continued their tour, the group passed by a small playground containing a few swings, a slide, and a whirly bird. A boy around seven or eight sat on the swing, very still, with an unhappy expression. That look was a familiar one to Ben—a look of hopelessness and the acceptance that life is cruel.

Ben walked over to the boy and asked if he wanted a push. The boy, so unused to a friendly overture, had no immediate response, so Ben gently pushed the swing for a few minutes.

The motion de-stressed the boy. Upon hearing the word, "higher," Ben happily complied. For a few minutes this needy child experienced a bit of joy. When the group moved on, Ben told the boy that if he was still there when the tour was finished Ben would push him on the whirly bird.

The group had already reached the cottage by the time Ben caught up with them. He had never seen the building before. The place intrigued him even though it was in dire need of paint and had several lopsided or missing shutters. As he stepped inside to join the group, Ben felt that this house was calling him to investigate all it offered.

Ben fell in love with what he saw and with the potential that he could only see in his mind's eye. Here was a place to start a purposeful singular life. Finding Marge in the middle of the tour group, he told her he would be by the playground. The young boy was still there. When he saw Ben coming, he ran to the whirly bird.

When the tour was over, Ben asked if he could talk privately to the manager. Within an hour Ben had a new home and a meaningful role in life. He would take the paltry salary Lou Harden offered. In return he would use his skills to maintain the shelter. Besides paying the rent, Ben often used his own money to enhance the children's lives.

# Chapter 29

By the following spring, a remarkable change had occurred at Drayton House, at least on the outside. Daffodils and tulips and all the other harbingers of the season transformed the property from neglected to eye-catching. People in the area stopped their cars as they drove by. They couldn't believe the difference. Walkers paused to admire the view. Previously, they would pass that dismal building as quickly as possible, without giving it a second glance.

Inside the shelter, a totally different scenario was playing out. Lou Harden's top priority was to supplement his own finances. Whenever he could use state funds to line his own pockets, he went for it.

Lou had zero compassion for the young victims that arrived at the shelter or for his employees. Practically all the workers were desperate for jobs. They had serious problems of their own and so took little notice of what was going on within the walls of Drayton.

Most of the shelter children were temporary placements. Shortly after arrival, they realized little was done to ease their mental anguish. The rare visits with social and psychological personnel fell short in reaching the disenchanted. The one light in their brief stay at the shelter was the man in the cottage.

In the winter Ben provided sleds for fun on the small hill in back of his house. He also set out warm cups of cocoa on a picnic table at the bottom of the hill. The spring season brought with it activities such as preparing the garden and playing baseball. Ben made sure a croquet set was always out on the lawn. He would also help kids with homework while serving homemade cookies.

Summer was the ultimate time for outdoor pleasure. The playground was now equipped with safe and imaginative toys. Ben built a small train and a house with a table and chairs. Outside the playground area, a tree house provided a private getaway for a single child at a time, since it was only big enough for one.

As the fruit and vegetables ripened, the children picked them from the garden and enjoyed healthy snacks. Discipline was unnecessary. The children knew that if they didn't act properly, they would not be invited to participate in the fun. Children can pick out insincerity. Ben was honest and caring, and thus he became the oasis in their bleak lives.

Lou Harden held the upper hand within the walls. The hapless children were the losers. Food was of poor quality, and hand-me-down clothes were given to the children while they were there. Rumors flew among the staff suggesting that Lou Harden had sexually assaulted a young girl working in the kitchen. Employees noted he gaped at her constantly.

One particular story was certainly cause for investigation, but unfortunately, it never reached ears that would listen. One of the workers was on her way home one evening but realized she had left her sweater at the shelter. Upon reaching the kitchen, she heard banging noises in the pantry. As she got closer, sounds of distress reached her ears. Frightened, she quickly took off and called a fellow worker. That woman told her to forget about it or she would lose her job. The girl purported to be the victim never returned to work. Actually, she was never seen again.

This was the setting in which three-year-old Marie began her new life. Refusing to divulge any information other than her first name, Marie barely interacted with anyone at the shelter. And so some of the workers and other children thought she was retarded.

No one came forward with any background information about Marie, and since she continued to play her act of being ignorant, a judge had to label her as "unadoptable." And thus she became a long-time resident of Drayton.

The lack of compassion at the shelter was no surprise to Marie. She had never experienced nurturing attention in her short life. She learned at a young age to trust no one and protect herself. Keeping out of sight was usually a safe policy.

Marie met Ben soon after her arrival at Drayton. She went right to the puzzles as well as the drawing materials set up outside the cottage. When Ben asked her a few questions, her responses were limited to one word. He knew this was her self-protection so he dropped the questioning. When he brought her juice and a cookie, she thanked him but her expression remained emotionless.

After Marie went inside, Ben picked the most decorated box he had and wrote "Marie" on it in calligraphy. A small drawing personalized this container that was to be the receptacle of Marie's creations.

Another day Marie was the first one to arrive. Ben handed her the box with her name. She murmured a thank you, her expression belying the pleasure this simple gift created. Soon the box overflowed with Marie's handiwork. Whenever Ben read to the children, Marie sat right at his feet. Still no dialogue was exchanged.

Marie's communication with the staff was so limited the people at Drayton were convinced she had a low IQ. The only problem with this theory was her immediate and accurate response to directions. This was reported to the Child Study Team. Ben spoke to the group, suggesting they observe her capabilities.

# Chapter 30

Meetings between the Child Study Team and the Drayton staff took place once a month. The object was to share details about each child and then develop a plan to improve the children's stay at Drayton. The Child Study Team had spent time together evaluating each child's situation, so they arrived at the Drayton shelter well prepared for their monthly appointments.

The fact that their recommendations fell on deaf ears disappointed them each month. It was frustrating to know that these sessions had very low priority for the Drayton staff, with the exception of one participant. Ben always brought the children's boxes to these meetings, and his insights about the children were right on target. But the problem was that there was little Ben could do as far as changing any policies at Drayton.

The one with the least interest was Lou Harden. His contribution about each child was usually a rehash of the information provided when the child had arrived at Drayton. Lou spent more time looking at his watch than contributing anything worthwhile.

One of the questions asked of the children at their interviews was who made them smile. Without a moment's hesitation, the answer was the same. The children adored Ben. When asked about someone who made them sad, Lou Harden always came up, except they just called him the man in the office. They didn't know his name.

At first the team reported these comments to the state, but Lou must have found out about the complaints. At a later interview one child blurted out that he had hit them and took away a week of Ben's sessions. At the next monthly meeting Ben also spoke about this situation to one of the team members when Lou was occupied elsewhere. Ben noted that Lou was a detriment, not an asset, to the shelter. But it wasn't easy removing and replacing shelter managers. Qualified applicants were not interested as the salary was not commensurate with what the job entailed. Often the only ones applying were greedy, self-centered individuals just like Lou.

At a meeting held a few weeks after Marie's arrival at Drayton House, the little girl's evaluation was the main topic. Since Marie was labeled an "unadoptable" and would probably end up staying at Drayton until she was of age, it was important to assess her abilities and potential and make some kind of plan for her future. When Marie's name came up, the staff all seemed to agree that she had limited capabilities. However, they also acknowledged that Marie completed directions without needing explanation.

Ben waited until everyone who wanted to contribute had been given the opportunity to talk. Unfortunately, Rose Romero, the Shelter Coordinator, was at a meeting off site that day and so she could not comment. Rose was the only other staff member who had noticed Marie's abilities, the only other person who would back Ben up.

When everyone had finished, Ben cleared his throat, stood up slowly, and began to address the group. "I have to disagree with this evaluation of Marie. I am not a teacher, but I have spent a lot of time with the children at Drayton. I find Marie to have amazing talents and abilities, far above what is expected from one so young. I know she doesn't communicate well, but I have the gut feeling that she is protecting herself."

As a detective, Ben had reported on cases where the consequences affected lives. He spent hours making sure his words were accurate, not only with the facts of the case but all the background circumstances of both the victim and the accused. Judges found his testimony to be honest and straightforward. They were pleased whenever he was called to testify. Now Ben addressed the Child Study Team in the same forthright manner.

When Ben opened Marie's box, jaws dropped. The box contained a variety of items created by a very gifted child: drawings, sketches, Lego constructions, clever items made with material and ribbons. One female staffer said she didn't believe these had been done by Marie. Ben did not verbally refute her criticism. Instead, he continued to support his evidence.

"Yesterday, I decided to take the plunge and try to find out why she wasn't talking. We were picking carrots for dinner. I told her that she wasn't fooling me. I knew that she was smarter than most children her age and even older. But I pointed out that her silence would work against her. If she didn't talk to people, they wouldn't realize how bright she was or know what her interests were. She might miss out on doing lots of wonderful things that she was capable of doing.

"I asked her if she trusted me. She said she did. Then I promised not to tell anyone else anything about her unless I had her permission."

One of the other staffers interrupted. "Well, you are a liar. You're telling us about her now."

Ben asked that she wait until he finished before judging him, and then continued. "It took awhile before Marie responded. Finally she shared a frightening story about being abandoned by her mother but was careful not to name any people or locations. She said her mother would kill her if she told anyone about her family. It took some time, but I finally convinced her that I was only interested in letting people know about her abilities so we could help her.

"I'll have more information to add to this after we hear what the team has to report."

The team spokeswoman opened with a statement that shocked Drayton's staffers.

"Ben, you always make our group want to do more. You set a standard that everyone should aim for but probably will never achieve. Your insight, dedication, and love of children are remarkable. How lucky Drayton House is to have a defender of children like you."

Ben was taken completely by surprise. This man who normally had no problem communicating was at a loss for words. He did manage to mumble an embarrassed "thank you" though.

The rest of the Drayton staff had to applaud, even though his success made them look like losers. Lou Harden was seething. While everyone was clapping, he snuck out of the room and retreated to his office.

As soon as the spokeswoman for the Child Study Team began the report on their findings, it was obvious that Ben was right on target. During their interview with Marie, the child had answered their questions in complete sentences as long as the subject did not pertain to her personal history.

Another team member who was a psychologist revealed amazing examples of Marie's mental abilities. "During the testing, Marie was first seated at a table set up with puzzles along with problem solving activities without directions. The test was geared toward a three-to-five-year-old child. It was timed, but Marie was not aware of that. The psychologist merely told her to finish as much as she could. The time limit for the team to make a judgment was twenty minutes.

"We went out of the room so we wouldn't intimidate Marie. Eight minutes later she came out of the room asking for the bathroom. We said she could finish her test when she got back. Her answer was a simple, 'I *am* finished.'

"At first we were disappointed because we figured she couldn't have completed enough of the test for us to evaluate her abilities, but we were shocked when we saw that she actually had finished everything."

Another member of the Child Study Team added: "We were dumbfounded when we took note of her accomplishments. She had finished all the projects without any errors.

"One of the problem situations had four sections. The first block showed a man picking tomatoes. The second had a man paying for the items at a store. The third block showed the man cooking the tomatoes. The fourth block was empty.

"The object was to pick the correct picture from three choices. One had the man sleeping, another showed him dancing, and the last showed him at a table eating. Marie not only chose the correct picture but she also made a drawing on the back of the paper showing children sitting at a table eating. The drawing was so detailed that we all could tell it was the table in front of Ben's cottage.

"The team then tested her reading. They discovered that she read on a third-grade level. However, when someone read to her, her comprehension was on a sixth-grade level."

Concluding their report, one of the members proposed that the next step was to design an education plan for this gifted child. State funding and scholarships were available for children like Marie. In the meantime, perhaps Ben could work with Marie using materials the team would supply.

Lou crept back into the room just in time to hear the team's proposal. He immediately snapped that Ben would not have the time.

Ben was furious with Lou's comment since the manager wasn't even there for the majority of the team's report. But he had to swallow any negativism if he wished to be a part of the children's lives.

No one picked up on his forced smile as Ben replied, "I think we can work something out, Lou."

There was little Lou could do without embarrassing himself, so he chose the non-committal response, "Perhaps."

Before the meeting concluded, Ben asked if he might bring Marie in to give additional evidence to add to the team's findings. At first the team was concerned with the suitability of it, and the Drayton staff had heard enough about this brilliant child they had labeled as a slow learner. They already felt embarrassed by their inability to probe beyond Marie's outward behavior.

Ben assured them that Marie liked the idea of talking with them as long as no one asked about her past, and the group finally agreed to talk with her. Ben brought the three year old in and seated her right next to him.

Ben announced, "Marie would first like to sing a song called 'Castle on a Cloud.'" Her sweet voice and perfect enunciation brought tears to everyone's eyes. The young girl from *Les Miserables* and Marie were both abandoned children.

Marie continued to illustrate her capabilities with poise and ease. She named US state capitals, oceans of the world, and zodiac signs. She ended by reading two pages from *Winnie-the-Pooh*, a children's classic that Ben had found in Drayton's small library of children's books that someone had donated. After Marie had finished reading, there wasn't one individual in that room who questioned that she was a prodigy.

After that meeting, Ben was mentoring not only Marie but every child who was temporarily placed at the shelter. To cut down his own workload so that he would have more time to spend with the children, Ben personally hired a part-time maintenance assistant and paid him using his own money. Amir was a college student from Pakistan who was enrolled in a new field of microbiology aimed at feeding Third World countries with nutritious grains produced cheaply and abundantly. The young man was an asset in every way, anticipating fix-it jobs before being asked. In spite of his busy schedule, Amir also found time to play sports with the children.

Thanks to the efforts of the Child Study Team and Ben, Marie, at the age of six, was accepted into a special program for the highly gifted at the same state university Amir attended. And the school was only seven miles away from Drayton. Ben and Amir took turns providing Marie's transportation. Ben saw to it that Marie had nice clothes and money for her expenses.

Unfortunately, several of the shelter's staff members were resentful of the preferential treatment they felt Marie received. They were often abusive to her, both mentally and physically. Marie avoided talking to them, so they thought she felt superior to them. In fact, the opposite was true. Marie was a kind and thoughtful child. But she was acutely afraid of the staff and had bruises to prove that she was justified to be scared of them.

She never revealed the abuse and hid her black-and-blue marks under her clothing. This made the staff believe they could continue mistreating her. If only Marie had told Ben, Amir, or the Child Study Team, the abuse would have ended. But children often let fear conquer reason.

# Chapter 31

Drayton's manager, Lou Harden, created an even more unpleasant atmosphere at Drayton House. He was getting careless, filling his pockets rather than using the money earmarked for the children. Cutting salaries, planning cheap meals, and short changing the shelter revealed neglect. The state employees representing children finally became aware of the situation.

Ben mentioned the manager's lack of honesty and integrity to various responsible caseworkers, but he didn't want to go too far with his accusations without proof. However, the proof soon presented itself, as often happens when a guilty person becomes remiss. Lou got away with chicanery for so long that he lost all caution.

One day the cook went into Lou's office to leave her supply order for the kitchen. He always insisted on purchasing everything himself at the same small grocery store.

Lou was not in his office, so she put the list on his desk. As she did so, she couldn't help but notice that papers were strewn all over, which was most unusual for a man who liked to keep everything under lock and key. The cook saw a bill from the grocery from the previous month, all itemized with products and prices.

The cook had always suspected Lou of swindling state money. She had a good idea of his salary range, and it did not correspond with his life style. He owned an expensive car and was also known as a big-ticket spender.

But even though she had been suspicious, what the cook saw on Lou's desk not only astounded but appalled her as well. The bill from the grocery had thirty-five items. The cook recognized fifteen of them. The twenty other items included cuts of prime meat, dairy, produce, cooking supplies, cleaning products, and other items that Drayton House never received.

After reading this, the cook began flipping through the other papers. There was a bill for a new couch, another for outside building repairs. There was no new couch, and Ben and Amir did all the building repairs except for major repairs, such as a new roof.

The cook immediately looked for Ben to show him what she had discovered. While Lou's cheating was no surprise to Ben either, the amounts and the unscrupulous way he managed to fill his coffers while cheating children and the state shocked Ben. And what he and the cook had seen was only one month's set of bills

They concurred that they had to do something immediately. First Ben contacted the Director, who assured Ben that he would immediately send out the local police with a search warrant. Meanwhile, he advised Ben to lock Lou's office. If possible, the police would enter the house without the Manager's knowledge, search the room and seize the incriminating papers, and then arrest him.

Lou drove up to the house before the police arrived and before Ben had turned off the lights in his office. Panicking at the thought of anyone seeing his paperwork, Lou parked his car several blocks away, behind an unoccupied building, and then raced through back yards, finally crouching behind a tree that had a clear view of the shelter.

Within minutes, an unmarked car parked a block away from the shelter. Somehow the detectives in the car managed to enter the shelter without Lou seeing them. An hour later, he was still hiding behind the tree, anxiously watching for any activity inside. But the house was dark, which was unusual.

Lou made the decision to take off when he saw a car with official plates pull up in front of the shelter. Something was definitely going on. Planning a permanent escape needed serious deliberation. He only had a limited amount of cash on him, so he would have to clean out his bank account before the police realized the magnitude of his crime.

Lou wasted no time getting back to his car. Driving down residential side streets, he finally turned into a lot and parked in a partially hidden corner. He spent the rest of the night sitting in his darkened car, mentally working over scheme after scheme. He finally decided to go to the bank as soon as it opened, hoping the investigation hadn't yet progressed beyond the bills at the shelter.

At 9 a.m. the next morning, Lou Harden entered the bank. It was most important to him that he not appear suspicious. He slowly opened the door and gave a warm good morning to the guard before walking straight to a familiar teller. He presented her with a withdrawal slip for almost his entire savings, except for the five hundred dollars necessary to keep the account open.

Worried that she might ask him why he was withdrawing such a large amount, he explained, "I'm buying a house and I am getting a much better price by paying cash."

The teller had no reason to doubt him, but she suggested Mr. Harden pay with a treasurer's check, which would be safer than carrying all that cash around.

"No, I can't do that. Cash was the deal."

Later that day when the news broke that Lou Harden was a fugitive from the law, the teller realized why cash had been so important to him. But by then Lou had been driving for several hours, trying to distance himself as far as possible from Drayton House.

# Chapter 32

A few weeks later, Lou was in South America, basking in the sun and his good luck.

He had doctored his bill of sale for his high-priced car and made sure that the used car lot and the salesman were the seediest possible. He offered to sell the car at a price the salesman couldn't resist. To sweeten the pot, Lou bought a fairly recent model car without questioning the price.

They both knew Lou was in a hurry to close the deal. Instead of questioning how legal the deal was, the salesman was already planning how he would spend his commission. Lou waited a few minutes and then pulled five brand new one-hundred-dollar bills from his wallet.

Making sure no one else could overhear their conversation, Lou took a step closer to the salesman and quietly pushed his plan. "This money is for you if you make sure my name doesn't appear on any documents we put together. And I want to see proof."

The salesman quickly gathered up all the paperwork and disappeared for about fifteen minutes, leaving Lou waiting in his office. When he came back, he brought several sales documents with him. Grinning broadly, he laid them out on his desk before Lou. A woman's name appeared on all of them.

As Lou finished signing the documents, his grin matched the salesman's. "Very nice doing business with you."

"Ditto," replied the salesman.

The next hurdle was to get across the Mexican border without a passport. Then he would head for Brazil. Lou never had trouble finding people of his own ilk. In Arizona, by taking his time to find the right person to help him, he managed to get a fake passport.

He then sold the car he had just purchased and made his way, by various means of transportation, to Brazil.

Lou's only regret was having to leave his main cache behind at the shelter.

Before Lou went to work for the shelter, he had been an assistant to the local coroner. His father was coroner for the city when Lou was young. He had been well respected throughout his entire career, which paved the way for an easy slide into a good career for his son.

As an assistant to the coroner, Lou listened to the police monitor day and night. He often arrived before the first responders. He would snatch jewelry from anyone who was unconscious. If people stopped to help they thought he was making an attempt to save lives. He was able to get away with this for several years and had amassed a collection of jewelry worth a fortune. Now that he was in South America he could easily sell the pieces—if he had them to sell.

When he was hired by Drayton House, Lou spent days looking for a spot to hide his stockpile. There was a room once used as a library that was near his office. Now it only served as a storage room for some of the original furniture no longer in use.

An old grandfather clock stood silent among the pieces, but at its base was a drawer. Lou always carried the key to that drawer with him. He spent some time adding a false compartment just above that drawer. Lifting the edges with a screwdriver was the only way to open the secret compartment. This inventive idea protected his booty from being discovered.

At some point, Lou would return to collect what he considered rightfully his.

# Chapter 33

Marie's life took a positive turn during the next several years. The University School for the Gifted was exactly where she needed to be. By the age of sixteen she had completed her high school requirements and had earned two years of college credits. Starting in September, she would be attending the University on a full scholarship.

Mrs. Andrews, Lou Harden's replacement, offered her the chance to remain at Drayton House until she was ready to move into a dorm room. During the summer Marie took an early afternoon class at the University and also spent two hours a day tutoring the shelter children. When they completed their lessons, she let them choose from a variety of craft projects.

Marie's life held great promise, especially for an unadoptable child with such a traumatic beginning. She and Ben were never at a loss for conversation whenever they were together. But one afternoon when Ben arrived to pick her up, he seemed a bit preoccupied.

The school had cancelled afternoon classes to allow students to attend a well-known author's presentation. Ben wondered why Marie hadn't gone. Marie replied that she didn't much care for the author, and she had to prepare for an important exam the next day. By leaving school now, she would have a few hours to study before the shelter children were ready for her.

Marie noticed that Ben wasn't as enthusiastic as usual and asked if anything was bothering him.

"Marie, I had the strangest incident happen this morning. I don't even know if I am completely off base. I certainly hope I am. After picking up the new door knobs for the upstairs rooms, I went to fill the van with gas. I went to a station I had never used before.

"After filling up, I went inside to pick up a newspaper. As I opened the door, I almost ran into a man who was wearing a scarf that covered half his face. You know how warm it was today, so that was odd by itself. But on top of that, although I couldn't see his whole face, he really reminded me of Lou Harden."

Marie asked who Lou Harden was. Ben had forgotten how young Marie was when Lou disappeared, so he filled her in on how Lou had been using state funds meant for Drayton House to buy things for himself. It had been eleven years since Ben had avoided the trap police had set for him.

Marie wondered, "After all that time, why would he come back? Did he leave anything behind?"

"Not that I know of," Ben replied. Then he dropped the subject. Even if it were Lou, the last place he would show up would be Drayton, so he didn't want to upset Marie.

As he let Marie off in front of the shelter, he mentioned that the local Women's Club had taken the younger children to a local museum for the day. Since they wouldn't be back until late afternoon, Mrs. Andrews sent the staff off on errands and she went to see her daughter. Ben was on his way to pick up some paint but would be back by dinner. He was going to barbecue veggies and put together a vegan dish Marie loved.

"You mean I have the whole place to myself all afternoon? Hooray! I can study in silence!" Marie exclaimed as she hopped out of the car.

# Chapter 34

Marie entered the shelter through the back door. As she reached the large main room, she saw a man carrying a tote bag coming out of the small adjacent room. He looked like he was making off with some sort of loot, but there wasn't anything of value in the shelter.

As Marie was trying to make sense of the situation, the man lunged at her, knocking her on the floor and pitching his body against hers. She struggled to get up, but he swung the tote bag at her head.

*This must be Lou Harden,* Marie thought just before she blacked out.

What should he do with the girl? He knew time was not on his side. The shelter was rarely empty, so he had to hurry before someone came in on him.

Lou dragged the girl back into the small room. She was regaining consciousness but was still groggy. The floor was littered with fragments of wood and glass, the remains of the grandfather clock that had housed his treasure. Lou maneuvered the moaning girl around the fragments and dropped her in a corner of the room.

After closing the door, Lou rummaged through the cabinets looking for some tape to cover the girl's mouth and something he could use to tie her up. While his back was turned, Marie pushed herself up off the floor. She was running for the door when he tackled her.

Lou pushed her so hard that he could hear the cracking sound of broken bone as her body slammed down on the floor. As Marie screamed in agony, Lou pulled a revolver from his jacket.

# NICHOLAS

# Chapter 35

The name Craig Farrow only existed in the memory of his sister Jenny. Nicholas Garlow grew up never knowing about his past. Unfortunately, the young boy was totally unaware there was someone who always was thinking of him. He was only four months old when Jenny had last seen him, but she had never forgotten his precious smile.

The attendants in the nursery of the foundling home where he was first placed adored the beautiful, sweet baby boy. Nicholas stayed there for two years. Everyone at the home was amazed at his developmental ability. He sat up, crawled, walked, and spoke far earlier than any other child who had ever been there.

Unfortunately, a little boy's fate was determined by the careless mistake of a clerk. No one had been able to discover anything about Nicholas' history. The state was reluctant to place a child up for adoption if the background was unclear, and their concern was reasonable. If the biological parent turned up at some future date claiming the child, the upheaval to the child and the adoptive family could be devastating. And yet shouldn't it have been worth the risk when the alternative was growing up in a shelter?

When Nicholas was two years old, he was transferred to an orphanage. The first few years after he left the nursery facility he was an easy child to manage. At times he would be assigned to a home for a single night, but his stay was often extended for weeks or more. However, at a very young age, Nicholas became conscious of the disparity between how the temporary foster parents treated their own children and the way they treated him. A child needs love and protection. Nicholas received neither.

The bulk of the emotional damage occurred to Nicholas between the ages of four and ten. In one temporary home he was bullied by the oldest biological child, who taunted Nicholas by reminding him that he didn't really belong there. At another home, his temporary parents took away his favorite toy to discipline him. At still another place, he didn't get as much to eat as the biological children did. Nicholas was always hungry, and so he would grab bread, crackers, anything that was left over on a table and horde it in his coat pockets. But then one of the other kids would tattle on him, and his punishment would be to go without dinner.

By the age of seven, Nicholas was a sullen, crafty child. His personality certainly could not be termed "endearing." About this time, he began to steal small items from his classmates. There was such a negative aura around Nicholas that no adult or child wanted to associate with him.

Teachers noticed he had potential, but Nicholas took no interest in school. He rarely completed his homework, and his class participation was nil. On the other hand, he read constantly and did extremely well on his regular tests without ever studying.

# Chapter 36

During the Christmas holiday, the orphanage would close for two days, giving the staff time to be with their families. This meant that all the children who stayed at this facility had to be placed in foster care for a two-night stint. Nicholas was, of course, the most difficult child to place, but he was finally assigned to a new family that had recently signed up to be part of the foster program. The father had lost his job and this was a way to supplement their income. Before Nicholas left the orphanage, he was warned that if he misbehaved, he might be transferred to the children's detention facility. Children who spent time at the orphanage knew this was a place to be avoided.

Early on Christmas Eve, Nicholas arrived at a household that already had issues. He recognized one of the boys from his school—Brian. Nicholas was several grades ahead in math and was placed in Brian's class for that subject. Nicholas' ability irked the boy, who took every opportunity to mock him. Since Brian was a lot bigger than he was, Nicholas' only resort was to withdraw into his own world. Soon Brian's brother began to pick on Nicholas too.

Every time the boys were alone with Nicholas they took the opportunity to verbally taunt him as well as physically push him around. Even when the parents were nearby, the boys didn't include Nicholas in anything.

The evening seemed endless. The boys were so excited about Christmas that sleep was not on their agenda. It was after midnight when they finally quieted down.

Awakened by whooping and screaming at 6 a.m. the next morning, Nicholas rushed downstairs to join the family. He knew there was a present for him from the orphanage and had been hoping for a Lego set. The more complex the set, the more it appealed to him.

The parents wished him a Merry Christmas and then switched their attention back to their own children. After they had opened several presents, the father handed Nicholas a large box with his name on it.

Nicholas knew who had chosen his present. A social worker who visited with the children three days a week knew how much he loved building. As he unwrapped the gift, suddenly all the ugliness of the night before was forgotten. Underneath the wrapping paper was a huge box of Legos, the exact set he had seen in the magazine he had shown the social worker. He could build lots of neat things with this set!

One of the other boys noticed the amazing Lego set and started to tease Nicholas. "Oh sure, like a little punk like you could build anything. That set says it's for ages fourteen and older. You're seven. What a stupid gift."

The mother half-heartily admonished her son while announcing that breakfast was ready. Nicholas didn't feel like eating. All he wanted to do was work with the best present he had ever received. The family was not unhappy eating without him. The mother brought him a piece of toast and a glass of milk and moved his present to a card table in the den.

Excited to start building, he began to check out all the wonderful projects he could make. After choosing one of them, Nicholas looked over the plans and pulled out the pieces he would need. For the next few hours, Nicholas was in a world where only he and his blocks existed.

Eventually the mother came in to check on Nicholas. When she saw what he had built, she looked at him in astonishment. "Did you make that?"

"Yup," Nicholas responded.

Amazed that a seven year old was capable of such complexity, she ran out of the room and came back shortly with her husband, dragging him in to look at what she thought impossible for such a young boy. Her husband was flabbergasted.

On the table stood a Ferris wheel, complete with seats as well as a switch that propelled the wheel into motion. Both adults were totally astounded that anyone, let alone a seven-year-old child, could complete a project like that in just a few hours. They both complemented Nicholas, and as he thanked them a tiny hint of a smile crossed his usually sullen face.

The couple called their boys in to see this impressive achievement. This rubbed salt into Brian's feeling of inadequacy. His school achievements were poor. School subjects came slowly for him, and he always struggled. Nicholas never talked in school, never did homework, yet he received perfect grades on tests.

Brian's Christmas was ruined. He said nothing, forgetting the euphoria of Christmas morning. Slowly he walked away from the detestable object.

# Chapter 37

Nicholas went to the bedroom and slowly got dressed. He dreaded spending the rest of the day and night with the boys—especially Brian. He could only hope that Brian would be so busy with his new toys that he would leave Nicholas alone. He held on to that thought as he walked back downstairs.

Returning to the den to take another look at his handiwork, Nicholas gasped in horror. Pieces of the broken Ferris wheel were scattered all over. Its motor lay smashed on the floor. Obviously, someone had stomped on it over and over. The boy's gasp quickly turned into a raging howl as his small body shook with grief.

The family rushed into the den—all except Brian. He was nowhere to be seen. The parents guessed what had happened but had no idea what to do. Horrified to see a child in such torment, they immediately called the manager of the orphanage, who had given them an emergency number where she could be reached. When the manager answered her phone, the spine-chilling shrieks reached her ears before the father could say anything.

A few minutes later, the screaming ceased abruptly. Nicholas became quiet and lethargic. His face and lips turned pale. When the mother asked him if he was OK, he said he felt dizzy and kind of weak. She realized he was going into shock and told her husband and the manager that they needed to call 911 right away.

The traumatized child fought as the EMS responders tried to secure him into a gurney. When one of the paramedics heard that the broken Ferris wheel had caused the boy's meltdown, he grabbed the box, collected as many of the scattered pieces as he could, threw them into the box, and put it on the gurney. He told Nicholas that it was OK—the Ferris wheel could be fixed. Finally Nicholas calmed down enough for the paramedics to put him onto the gurney next to his precious box.

When they heard Nicholas was from the local orphanage and that a boy from the household had destroyed his Christmas present, all of the emergency responders reached into their pockets and donated enough money for a brand new set. All the way to the hospital the kind paramedic repeated that Nicholas was going to have all the pieces from his first set plus a brand new set.

Traumatic episodes do not subside easily. The boy still exhibited symptoms of shock when the ambulance arrived at the hospital. He was vomiting and had cold and clammy skin; a quick, weak pulse; rapid, shallow breathing; and bluish lips.

The attending doctor expressed concern, so the ashen boy was wrapped in heated blankets and given an intravenous solution to hydrate and calm him. In the meantime, the manager of the orphanage arrived at the hospital. She had called the social worker who had bought Nicholas the present. Shortly after, the woman and her husband walked in.

The social worker began to cry as she related what she knew about the boy: "Nicholas is extremely intelligent but filled with despair. He has no friends and is a loner. He showed me a picture of this wonderful Lego set that he saw in a magazine. It was expensive and he knew no one would buy it for him. He talked about it and it became almost an obsession with him. When I told my husband about it, he suggested we buy Nicholas the set for Christmas."

Nicholas responded well to treatment he was given at the hospital, and by the next morning he was able to receive visitors. To his amazement, several paramedics paraded into his room, carrying what he thought was his very own Ferris wheel that had been magically put back together. Actually, they had bought a new set of Legos just that morning. But building the Ferris wheel had taken much longer than any of them had anticipated. It took four of them several hours. They could hardly believe that a little boy had built it in only a couple of hours.

Nicholas took one look at the Ferris wheel and his whole body relaxed. He lovingly stroked it and immediately fell asleep.

The next day the kindly paramedic called Brian's parents and asked if he could speak to their boy. They gave him permission, hoping the paramedic could help the boy see how cruel he had been to Nicholas.

"What's your name, son?

"Brian Kendall."

"Did you know Nicholas Garlow before he stayed at your house over Christmas?"

"Yeah, he comes into our class for certain subjects."

"What grade are you in?"

"Sixth"

"What grade is Nicholas in?"

"Second, but he's so smart. He does all the work we do faster. He makes us look stupid. My friends all hate him too. Our teacher makes a big deal about him. He doesn't talk to anyone. He thinks he's such a big shot. But he's nothing but a baby."

The paramedic got the picture. He could see where this kid was coming from. The whole situation had been handled miserably by Brian's parents, so he was going to try a non-threatening approach. He softened his voice and gently put his hand on the boy's shoulder as he pulled him over to the couch.

"What you did was terribly wrong, Brian. Destroying other people's property is against the law. That alone is a bad thing. How many presents do you think you got this Christmas?"

"Lots."

"Ten?"

"Much more."

"Which one was your favorite?"

"My new bicycle."

"Why do you think you received all these wonderful gifts?"

Brian thought a minute. He felt more comfortable talking to the stranger now.

"I guess because they love me."

"I know that's true. But not everyone is lucky enough to have parents that love them that much. I'd like to tell you something about Nicholas. Remember, he is only seven years old. When he was four months old, he was abandoned. He has never known a mother or father who could give him love or get him presents. The orphanage and some private organizations give the children gifts at Christmas, but they are limited as to how much they can spend.

"A social worker noticed the projects Nicholas had made with the old used blocks at the orphanage. When he showed her a magnificent Lego set in a magazine, her heart went out to the boy. She knew the Christmas presents he would receive would be well meant but inexpensive.

"The set Nicholas showed her contained complex diagrams of projects with motors. It was quite expensive. The second grader told her that he would buy that set when he grew up. She felt that if anyone deserved that present, it was Nicholas. And so she bought it for him.

"That set meant an awful lot to Nicholas. How do you think he felt when he saw what you had done to it?"

Brian was really a pretty good kid, but kids often act impulsively. Now he realized that what he had done was terribly wrong, and so he told his parents he wanted to apologize to Nicholas. They called the manager of the orphanage and arranged to bring their son over as soon as Nicholas was released from the hospital.

Brian wanted to give Nicholas something special. The bicycle was his favorite gift and he really loved it. As he and his parents were leaving for the shelter, Brian loaded the bike into the family's SUV. This amazed his parents, but no one was more surprised at this gesture than Nicholas.

When Brian offered his bicycle as a peace offering, all of the anger drained out of Nicholas. But he felt confused. Since he was only a small child, he couldn't understand how someone could cause him such pain one day and then give him such a great gift another day.

"I hate what I did to you. I really am sorry. I want you to have my bike. I'm sorry that I was mean to you in school too," Brian told the younger boy.

Nicholas was still bewildered but sensed Brian's sincerity. "I can't take your bike. That's your gift." He thanked Brian but became agitated as the conversation continued.

Brian's Mom broke into the conversation, trying to ease the tension. "Nicholas, Brian just wants to show you how sorry he is. Is there some reason you don't want the bike?"

Nicholas blurted out, "It would be stolen."

Brian suggested, "You could keep it at my house and come over anytime to ride it. I promise I won't touch it."

Acts of kindness can change lives. This is what happened with Nicholas. Even though there was a difference in age, a lasting bond was created between the two boys.

# Chapter 38

Nicholas still had years of loneliness ahead. However, a light began to shine into his dark world little by little, incident by incident. The horrific Christmas was a turning point in his life. And new people had become aware of his amazing ability.

As the years passed, he took advantage of every opportunity presented to him. His building creations expanded to the world of architecture. Academic awards provided him with an education, and business mentorships propelled him into a world of success.

Influenced by Nicholas, Brian also had a love of design. And when Nicholas went to work for a prestigious architectural firm, it didn't take long before Brian was working there too.

The two friends focused most of their time and energy on their careers; but in spite of their limited free time, they often managed to get together outside of work. That time usually was spent exploring technology. In the back of his mind, Nicholas had a vision of a mathematical formula that could be used to stabilize buildings against almost any destructive force. Brian listened with amazement as the intricacies of Nicholas' idea unfolded. As capable as Brian was in the same field, this concept was far beyond his scope.

Eventually, Nicholas pitched his concept to the partners at his firm. His mathematical formula to prevent building collapse would be programmed into computer software that still needed to be developed. But his vision could revolutionize the building industry and its benefits could be extended to Third World countries as well.

The company backed him up with a two-year research grant. If the program succeeded, Nicholas would pay the company a set amount as compensation. The corporation thought the price they set would reward them handsomely. They felt they had cinched a great deal. What a mistake! They should have required a percentage of the future success of the program!

A stint in Silicon Valley resulted in a program that catapulted Nicholas into billionaire status. After proper credit and remuneration were given to his architectural firm, Nicholas started his own firm with Brian as CEO. New York was their playground.

One of Nicholas' best decisions was hiring Claire, a woman in her late fifties who had recently retired as the CEO of Leviathan, a corporation that manufactured reinforced concrete. Claire had decided to retire before she met Nicholas. Money was not an issue, and she wanted the freedom to enjoy life without working constraints. She was an amazingly capable woman, able to manage career and family with admirable proficiency. *Admirable* is a fitting word because behind her efficiency was a warm, charitable nature. Few people were able to find fault with her, even if they did not totally agree with every one of her decisions.

The evening he first met Claire, Nicholas had invited his current steady girlfriend, along with Brian and his wife, to have dinner at the posh New York hotel Eldor. As they sat having drinks before dinner, Nicholas noticed a large group of formally dressed people gathered in a large room adjacent to the bar, which had been set up as a reception area. When he asked the bartender what the occasion was, he learned that it was a retirement party for the CEO of some company.

A few minutes later, Nicholas and his friends followed the maître d' to their table. On the way, he noticed a banner announcing "Leviathan Reception." Nicholas recognized the name of a giant corporation involved in construction.

Gourmet dining and animated conversation soon erased any thoughts about the Leviathan reception. The evening stretched on pleasantly until Nicholas' insecurities flared up. He started to feel like he didn't belong in these surroundings and didn't fit in with this group. He began to stuff rolls in his pockets, just as he had as a hungry child staying in temporary foster homes. He couldn't help himself. Brian noticed what he was doing and realized his friend's anxiety was getting out of control.

Suddenly Nicholas' date became repulsive to him. Beautiful as she was, she spent too much time talking about material things like designer clothes, travel to Europe, and luxury apartments. In his mind, she became a gold digger. Brian and his wife did not appear enthralled with her either, but they were being polite.

Nicholas regretted that he had reserved the hotel's top floor pent house for the night. Now all he wanted to do was go home to his new condominium on Park Avenue, alone.

As Nicholas' mood changed, Brian knew the evening was doomed even though it had nothing to do with him or his wife, Sara. His friend's date certainly wasn't helping with her inane chatter. Brian didn't know quite what to do, but this needed fixing.

When the two women got up to go to the restroom, Brian asked Nicolas what was wrong.

"Am I that obvious?"

"Nicholas, I've known you a long time now, and I can tell when something is bothering you."

"I can't take Ellen. I never realized that she was such a gold digger. I guess I should write this off as just one more failed relationship."

"Well, now you know, but that doesn't solve tonight's problem. You are getting rude. And you've been stuffing your pockets full of dinner rolls as well!"

Nicholas looked crestfallen. "I hope Sara isn't upset with me. I wouldn't hurt her for the world."

Brian reassured him that was not the case, but they hadn't been able to resolve anything before the women returned. A few minutes later Sara's cell phone vibrated. It was the babysitter calling to say their three-year-old daughter was throwing up and calling for them.

Brian and Sara apologized while Nicholas called for his driver to take them home. Brian knew this was an even worse turn for Nicholas since now Ellen was his only companion.

Once they were gone, Ellen retreated to their hotel room, claiming she'd had too much to drink. Nicholas had really hurt her feelings, but she didn't want to break off their relationship as he was a highly sought after catch. However, their lack of common interests was making it more and more difficult to find anything to talk about without Nicholas making nasty comments to her.

# Chapter 39

By now it was after midnight and the evening's events were winding down, but Nicholas wasn't ready to deal with Ellen. He wandered into the main bar, which was still pretty crowded. He had to admit that the room's decor was impressive, with a long antique bar as well as several sectional couches arranged in comfortable conversational groupings.

Nicholas looked lost sitting at one of these arrangements all by himself, but it gave him a chance to be alone with his thoughts, which were a combination of guilt, anger, and disappointment. Why did his past always turn into a cloud hanging over the present?

The party sitting at the grouping next to him laughed and chatted amicably. Nicholas nodded politely to a few of them. Whatever the occasion, it was certainly a happy one. Then, much to his surprise, the woman who seemed to be the center of attention got up from her seat, walked over to Nicholas, and sat down next to him.

"I'm Claire Talmadge, and I just had the best evening. Actually, I am still having a ball. You look like this evening was a disaster for you. Come join us and have a laugh or two. It's amazing what warm conversation can do to turn things around."

The woman had an engaging smile that made Nicholas feel comfortable.

"I'm Nicholas Garlow and I certainly don't want to impose my rotten mood on such a happy group, but thank you for your gracious offer. By the way, what are you celebrating?"

"I insist you join us and then you will find out!" Claire rose as she said this and offered Nicholas her hand.

Before they sat down, Claire introduced her newly acquired guest to the group. "Everybody, this is Nicholas Garlow. He needs a bit of cheering up, and I think we are all up to that. This is my husband,

Henry; our daughter, Kimberly, and her husband, Jason; and our son, Matthew. And last but certainly not least is my nephew Cal Reston and his wife, Jennifer. Cal is a board member of my favorite charity, Jennifer's Outreach. That completes our group. The happy occasion is the retirement party I was just given by the company where I worked, Leviathan."

Laughter rippled across the group as Matthew quipped, "Sure Mom, you just 'worked' at Leviathan. Actually, Mom was the CEO there, Nicholas."

Nicholas congratulated Claire and mentioned that he was familiar with Leviathan. His smile deepened as he began to enjoy himself and his new acquaintances. Two hours passed by quickly.

As Nicholas got ready to leave, Claire and Henry invited him to dinner the following Sunday. Matthew chimed in, explaining that his parents' Sunday dinners were wonderful occasions where new friends were most welcome. Normally wary of social invitations, Nicholas felt good about these people and graciously accepted.

When the waitress brought the bill, Nicholas insisted on picking up the tab. Henry tried to protest, but Nicholas had already sent the waitress off with his credit card, so everyone laughed and thanked him.

Nicholas looked up when the waitress came back to get his signature. Startled, she blurted out, "Wow, where did you ever get such spectacular green eyes?" When Nicholas frowned slightly, she realized her comment must have seemed forward. She apologized quickly and then disappeared with the signed credit card receipt.

Nobody paid attention to the waitress except Jennifer, Cal's wife. When she shook Nicholas' hand and said good night a few minutes later, she made it a point to look into his eyes.

As everyone scattered to their respective rooms, Claire insisted that Nicholas meet them for breakfast in the hotel dining room at 9 a.m.

Nicholas was about to enter the elevator when he did an about face, making his way to the front desk. He paid for the suite and told the night clerk to OK any additional costs Ellen might incur. Then he wrote a note and slipped it under her door:

*Ellen,*
*Sorry things didn't work out between us. It's entirely my fault. The bill is taken care of. Enjoy room service in the morning.*
*Nicholas*

When he got to his apartment, Nicholas felt upbeat even though he could not quite verbalize the emotion. He had lost out on a night with a beautiful girl and instead come home to an empty apartment. But he'd gotten enormous pleasure out of meeting some new people he truly enjoyed. Nicholas was not going to miss that breakfast!

# Chapter 40

"Great party!" Cal remarked as they walked into their hotel room.

It was a moment before Jennifer responded. "I felt so odd when Claire introduced Nicholas to us, but I can't figure out why." Then she shrugged and went into the bathroom to get ready for bed.

Cal was just nodding off when she rushed into the bedroom shouting, "Nicholas Garlow!"

It took several moments before Jennifer could arrange her garbled thoughts into some kind of logical order.

"Cal, Nicholas Garlow was the custodian at my school. I went to his funeral just before all hell broke loose at my house.

"And…. Did you hear the waitress mention Nicholas' green eyes? Craig had those same green eyes. And that's what started my whole family tragedy.

"Do you think he might be my Craig? He seems about the right age."

"Jen, you're jumping to conclusions. You want this so much that you're not thinking straight. Do you know how many people could fit the infant Craig's description as an adult? You haven't seen him since he was four months old."

Cal's logic did little to squelch the fire that had just been ignited. Jennifer was determined that Craig would be hers again, blotting out years of heartache.

Nicholas arrived at the hotel well before 9 a.m., making arrangements for a very special breakfast. The conversation was lively and animated, which enabled Jennifer to observe Nicholas without him noticing. Although she didn't say much to him, she hung on his every word, noting his facial expressions and the nuances of his voice.

After that breakfast, the friendship between Claire and Nicholas grew quickly. Claire was drawn to this successful young man who nevertheless seemed to be suppressing some deep inner discontent.

Within a few months Nicholas was a frequent guest at the Talmadges' Sunday dinners. He never appeared without his arms filled with gifts. Henry and Claire finally mentioned that while they appreciated his gifts, what they really enjoyed was his company. They suggested that he save his presents for the winter holidays and birthdays. Nicholas reluctantly agreed yet still found it hard to believe that he was just as welcome in their home if he showed up without any gifts.

During these visits Nicholas often asked Claire and Henry for advice. They discovered that this young entrepreneur was a genius when it came to groundbreaking technology, especially in the area of architecture and construction. As a result of his innovative architectural software, he was in a position to live without ever lifting a finger, buying anything he wanted and living anywhere in the world. He also had a well-balanced background in fine arts and literature. Amassing knowledge somehow lessened his feeling of inadequacy. But in spite of all his talents, he was at a loss concerning his future.

Spending time with the Talmadges became his Nirvana. He was beginning to understand what it felt like to belong. After numerous conversations with Henry and Claire, Nicholas decided that what he wanted was to construct notable buildings.

Brian was the CEO of his new company, but Nicholas was still looking for a CFO. Once he realized that Claire wasn't really ready for retirement, he convinced her to temporarily join them as CFO. Garlow and Associates was now ready to do business.

The one downside of Nicholas' new connection with the Talmadges had to do with Jennifer Reston. At first it was just annoying to find her starring at him when she thought he wasn't looking. But then she started to corner him unexpectedly and ask questions about his past. When the date of his birthday came up, he reverted to his aloof self-protective mode. It was difficult to even be casually friendly with her after that.

He finally mentioned his discomfort to Claire and Henry. They had never noticed anything odd; but now that Nicholas brought it to her attention, Claire recalled that Jennifer had asked her what she knew about his childhood.

At the next Sunday gathering, Jennifer headed straight toward Nicholas. After a brief greeting, she went into interview mode. Any reference to his childhood was torture to Nicholas, and he finally decided that he had had enough. Cal was standing nearby, so Nicholas asked him and Jennifer if he could speak with them in the library.

Jennifer's heart beat rapidly. Now the story would finally be revealed. Her lost baby brother with his sweet smile would gaze at her adoringly once again. All the years of pain and longing would soon be forgotten.

Sadly, the talk didn't go the way Jennifer hoped it would.

"Jennifer, you and Cal are nice people, and I hope we can continue to be friends. However, I can't be friends with you unless you stop asking me about my past. I have very few positive memories from my childhood, so I hope you can understand why I prefer not to discuss the past. I only live in the present and work for the future.

"Jennifer, I don't care if we are related in any way. I just don't want to go down that path."

Seeing that Jennifer was desperately trying to hold back tears, Nicholas apologized for his bluntness and quickly left the library.

Cal wrapped his wife in his arms and held her close to him. But after a moment she pulled away, and Cal noted a new look of determination on her face. Here was a different Jennifer, a phoenix rising above the ashes.

"That's it! This has been my grief. I've let it interfere with my life. You have been stuck with a wife that carried her childhood like a badge of martyrdom. Cal, you deserve better. For a long time, life with you has been the best. Nicholas is right. The past should be left in the past."

"You have never been a burden, Jenny, It hurt me to know how much you longed to reconnect with your lost baby brother when I didn't see how that would ever happen. I love you so much, Jenny. You mean everything to me."

That night, Jennifer stopped searching for her lost brother and started to live in the present.

.

# Chapter 41

Within two years, Nicholas' architectural firm was a permanent Manhattan fixture with an exclusive address. Claire was no longer temporary but worked full-time as CFO.

Nicholas lived in a magnificent apartment with everything imaginable at his disposal. His high-end refrigerator was loaded almost to overflow—he could probably survive for months on its contents. Yet he rarely ate at home, even though he employed a personal chef. Whenever the food got close to the perishable stage, it was donated to a food kitchen and the refrigerator was replenished. Nicholas would never find himself hungry again.

But all the fame and trappings of wealth could not erase a small boy's painful childhood memories of insufficient food and clothing, the lack of emotional support, the absence of family and of love.

Nicholas had broken off two engagements and was working on a third. He managed to back out of his engagements when his sense of panic overwhelmed him and brought everything to a standstill. The women were all from well-to-do, warm, and loving families who would have been more than happy to include Nicholas. His financial status still overrode his often-aberrant behavior. But if this handsome, wealthy, eligible bachelor had been just an ordinary person, potential brides would have dumped him as soon as his insecurities and bad behavior became obvious.

Nicholas was the epitome of charm, good looks, and intelligence blended with an uncanny ability to solve complex problems. In his professional life his behavior was consistent and logical. He was always poised and in control of every situation. But his personal life was another matter. He had put up an impenetrable wall that shut out anyone who asked too many questions about his past—including the women he had hoped to marry. Privacy was vital to his feeling of well-being. Losing control was not an option for him.

Claire handled his social as well as business obligations. Whenever Nicholas found himself trapped into a commitment he didn't want to keep, he depended on Claire to throw him a lifeline.

Now thirty-three years old, Nicholas wanted desperately to be married and have a family of his own. The women he had proposed to seemed to be women who could help him fulfill the image of family that he had built up in his mind. But then he always found some excuse to sabotage the relationship—it might be some imagined slight or perhaps a notion that the woman really just wanted his money.

Sue, fiancée number three, had the best record with Nicholas so far. A date for the wedding had been set and planning was well underway. Although he would have preferred something small but elegant, he let Sue and her family make lavish and extravagant arrangements. Sue came from a good family, and her parents were overjoyed at the prospect of having Nicholas as a son-in-law. But even though Sue was beautiful, intelligent, and loving, she had no more clue to the inner torment going on inside of him than any of his previous girlfriends had.

Claire was the only woman who suspected anything. She seemed almost clairvoyant when it came to picking up on a person's hidden fears and uneasiness. She sensed that Nicholas was a volcano about to erupt, although only she and his friend Brian had noticed the inner rumblings. Claire felt she knew what was behind Nicholas' turmoil but hesitated to discuss it with him for fear that he would shut her out too. When the time came and he finally asked for her help, she would be there to support him in any way that she could.

But right now Claire's attention was focused on her son, Matthew, who was the lawyer for Garlow and Associates. Matthew had recently met an attractive doctor from Ireland whose flaming red hair and compassionate nature made him fall madly in love.

A few years earlier, Siobhan had been working with Doctors Without Borders near the Afghan border. The stories she told him about her experiences revealed episodes of merciless inhumanity as humans

136

ignored the plight of victims escaping an intolerable existence. Siobhan was especially worried about her best friend, who was back there now and trapped in a hostile area. Siobhan hadn't been able to get any news about her friend for over two weeks and was growing more and more concerned for her safety. She had also contacted Ben, a dear friend from the shelter where Marie spent her childhood years. Ben hadn't heard from her in three weeks.

Claire and Henry were delighted with Matthew's charming new girlfriend, and they were concerned about Siobhan's troubling news in connection with her friend. Since Nicholas had so many international connections, Claire hoped he might be able to get an update on the whereabouts of Siobhan's friend, Marie.

News was hard to come by, but after several weeks Nicholas received some information from the area. The situation wasn't good. The land had been decimated by the fighting, and several local villages had been destroyed. Even though Marie's status was still unknown, authorities assumed the worst.

# MARIE

# Chapter 42

Instead of going to get paint after he dropped Marie off at the shelter, Ben decided to go back to the cottage to start dinner. As he peeled and cut up vegetables at the counter, he kept thinking about Lou. *If that really had been Lou at the gas station, why would he take such a risk? Was he coming back to Drayton House? Could he have left something there all those years ago?*

As he finished cutting the onions, Ben realized that he had forgotten to buy mushrooms. He walked over to the shelter, where he could borrow some. Halfway there he spotted a strange car in the driveway, which unnerved him. Had someone just stopped by, or had the car been there earlier? He hadn't noticed a car when he dropped Marie off, but that might have been because it was parked behind a clump of bushes to the side of the driveway.

Ben ran back into the cottage to call the shelter. He tried twice, but no one picked up the phone. Why wasn't Marie answering?

Realizing he was wasting valuable time, Ben dialed 911. When an officer answered, Ben quickly explained the situation.

"We're on our way!"

"Please hurry!"

Lou, completely involved with his immediate dilemma, had no idea that anyone had seen his car. He was aiming his gun at Marie when he heard the police at the front door. As they rushed into the shelter, Lou went on the defensive. Pointing his gun at the door, he fired at the first police officer to come in, shooting him in the leg. The officer returned fire, hitting Lou and killing him instantly. The tote filled with his precious jewelry lay next to his body.

Marie wasn't seriously hurt, but she did need a few stitches and stayed overnight in the hospital for observation. Meanwhile, the detectives started searching through their files to match the stolen jewelry with any old unsolved robberies. But since Lou had taken the pieces off of dead bodies, many of the robberies had gone unnoticed and thus unreported.

# Chapter 43

Marie's life moved on with successes and disappointments, as do most lives. Fortunately, the positives outweighed the negatives. Scholarships and grants paved the way to a successful career as a pediatrician. Her accuracy in complex diagnostic situations won praise from colleagues as well as her patients, and her empathy with distressed children enabled her to easily bond with her patients.

Marie worked four days at the Mt. Carmel Medical Center, which was located near Drayton House. A fifth day was devoted to volunteering at the Davidson Center, a trauma unit for troubled, neglected, or abused children located in Manhattan. This center bordered a very wealthy community but served the poor.

Marie and Siobhan were both pediatricians at Mt. Carmel, and Siobhan met Matthew Talmadge in the Emergency Room of that hospital. He was there with his sister, Kimberly, and his three-year-old niece, who had fallen out of her treehouse. Matthew was visiting when the accident happened and was the first to reach his niece, who had fallen onto her outstretched arm. Matthew thought she might have a broken collarbone, so he got the child and her mother into his car and drove directly to Mt. Carmel.

Matthew was immediately intrigued with the pretty redheaded doctor who spoke so softly to his niece as she gently examined the little girl. He loved her delightful Irish brogue too. Over the next few hours, he fell head over heels for her.

X-rays confirmed that Diane actually had broken her collarbone, so the doctor used a splint to wrap her shoulders and keep them in place and then put her arm in a sling. While the procedure was going on, both Claire and Jason, Kimberly's husband, arrived at the hospital.

By the time they were ready to leave the hospital, it was after seven and everyone was hungry. It was little Diane who suggested, "Let's go have wissghetti for my sore arm."

Claire called Henry, who was all for it, and they arranged to meet at a local Italian restaurant.

Matthew suggested they ask Nicholas and his fiancée to join them. Claire wished they could just invite Nicholas. While Sue was basically a nice person, Claire found her tendency toward one-upmanship in any conversation to be a bit off-putting. She knew the others felt the same way. Why was Nicholas so blind when it came to women?

Nicholas loved spending evenings with the Talmadges. Even though he saw Claire and Matthew every day, socializing was a totally different thing.

"Why in the world would you want me to tag along when you and Matthew have to take my abuse all day? You Talmadges must be gluttons for punishment," Nicholas teased when Claire invited him to dinner. "Let me check with Sue and I'll get right back to you."

The last thing Sue wanted to do was go to a family style Italian restaurant with people she didn't really like. There really was no reason for her to dislike the Talmadges. They went out of their way to include her. What really bothered her was the warm and easy relationship Nicholas had with this family. He never acted that way with her or her family.

Sue tried to get out of the dinner by listing all the wedding prep errands they had to do the next day. Nicholas' only comment was, "I'll have my driver pick you up. We're meeting them at Cianno's at eight."

Sue was furious, but Nicholas was the "Oscar" of bachelors, and she wasn't about to lose her prize.

As Claire finished her call to Nicholas, Kimberly asked her if she knew where Matthew was. After a few minutes of confusion, Matthew suddenly reappeared with a strange, light-hearted expression on his face.

"I've invited Dr. Innes to join us. I hope that's OK with everyone."

"Who?" asked a totally clueless Kimberly.

"Dr. Siobhan Innes, the doctor who took care of Diane."

Claire could barely contain her amusement. Matthew was considered to be the most conservative of the Talmadge family. Being impetuous was so out of character for him!

"Of course, dear. Since you have your car here, we'll meet you at Cianno's at eight."

"Don't say a word until we get to the car," Claire whispered to Kimberly.

Once they were in the car, mother and daughter burst into laughter. Poor little Diane had no idea what they were laughing about but it sounded like fun, so she joined in.

"That was fast!" Kimberly blurted out. "I'm sure it beats match.com."

"Maybe I should start looking for my 'Mother of the Groom' dress tomorrow."

"Don't order it online. It might arrive too late!"

When they got to the restaurant, Henry was waiting inside. As Claire gave him a quick kiss, she informed him that he was in for a shock and she would explain later.

Siobhan fit in easily with the Talmadge family and her relationship with Matthew bloomed quickly. After several weeks, people were already talking about the possibility of an engagement announcement coming soon. However, one problem threatened their bliss. Siobhan wished to return to Ireland and practice medicine in Dublin, not far from her home, but Matthew was ensconced with Garlow and Associates. The thought of starting over in a foreign land was not the least bit tempting to him.

Claire mentioned Matthew's bind to Nicholas, whose insight into other people's plights was often quite perceptive. He offered to buy them a house in Ireland that Matthew could also use as an office. Whenever he was needed in New York, he had the Garlow jet at his disposal.

The couple was overwhelmed by Nicholas' generosity, yet they hesitated to take him up on his offer. Given his upbringing and the example of his parents, Matthew's ethics made it difficult for him to accept what he considered unearned rewards. Siobhan's Irish upbringing mirrored similar principles.

Walking into Matthew's office without even a knock, Nicholas posed a question: "Matthew, do you love Siobhan or not, yes or no?"

"Of course I do. I never met anyone as wonderful as she. I don't know what I would do without her."

"Hmmmm. Are you certain she feels the same way?"

"Oh yes."

"If I felt that way about someone I would do anything to be with her. I have never been fortunate enough to experience the kind of love you two share."

"Sure, Nicholas, but you are in a financial situation where anything is possible. I haven't earned that status."

Nicholas changed his modus operandi. He really liked Siobhan, and he knew that Claire also believed the couple was deeply in love and right for one another.

"Matthew, who is your boss?"

"I don't know where you are going with this, but you are, of course."

"Do you like it here?"

"Of course."

"Then you either accept my offer or start looking elsewhere for a position. I'll give you a great letter of recommendation."

As Nicholas was leaving Matthew's office, he turned around in the doorway and added, "This does not apply to your mother. She's indispensable."

Once he was alone, Matthew couldn't help but grin. This was so typical of the way Nicholas did business: set the problem to its lowest denominator, then give a choice.

Matthew didn't have to mull it over. He concluded his life would never be complete without this woman who brought him such joy. Whatever it took, he was willing to adjust his aspirations to merge with hers.

# Chapter 44

Matthew left the office without a word and rushed across twenty blocks to the Davidson Center, where Siobhan was volunteering that day. He ran up the ten flights to the section where he thought she might be, not wanting to waste a moment waiting for the elevator.

Siobhan was sitting in the middle of a large room holding a crying toddler. Everyone else in the room turned as Matthew barged in. Even the crying child quashed her sobs.

"Siobhan, please marry me. I don't care where we live. I will go to the moon with you if that makes you happy."

Shocked, Siobhan couldn't react.

"Oh, for God's sake, marry the guy. Nobody gets proposals like that!" boomed a stentorian voice from a physician on her way to another floor.

"Of course, I'll marry you, Matthew. I never wanted to lose you. I don't know why location was so important."

After discussing Nicholas' offer at length, the couple talked to Claire, who pointed out the logic of the opportunity: "You've both worked hard for years; you're certainly not people who freeload or take advantage. Matthew, nowadays a person can work from anywhere. You don't have to be tied to an office in New York. Nicholas is one of the wealthiest men in the world. His generous gift would enable you and Siobhan to do the charitable services that are so important to you."

That sealed it. The couple graciously accepted Nicholas' offer and also started making wedding plans. But the date was not formally set as Siobhan wanted her best friend, Marie, to be her maid of honor.

Two years earlier, Siobhan had served with Marie in the same area where her friend was trapped now. It was near the Khyber Pass in Pakistan, close by the border with Afghanistan. When she tried to contact Marie using procedures they had used to call home on their previous trip, she couldn't get through.

The news Nicholas had been able to get was not good. Peshawar was in danger of being taking over by ISIL, and a serious earthquake had also been reported in the same area. This revelation put the couple's wedding plans on hold.

# Chapter 45

After graduating from high school back home in Ireland, Siobhan came to New York to attend medical school on a scholarship. She earned her medical degree and went on to get an advanced degree in pediatrics; afterwards she accepted a position at Mt. Carmel Hospital in a suburb near Manhattan. The Pediatric Intensive Unit became her home base, working with a team that included Marie Eaton.

The two young women became close friends. Both woman excelled in what they did, earning high regard from colleagues, other hospital staff, and patients. A concern for the wretched plight of the neglected and unfortunate was something else they had in common.

A few years after joining the Mt. Carmel medical team, they attended a talk by a representative of Doctors Without Borders, who presented a grim picture of a world desperate for medical assistance. Mt. Carmel was just one of the hospitals that had been approached about helping out with this crisis.

The Board of Directors offered to create portable medical containers packed so that the essential medical tools and medicines needed by a doctor were stocked in one compartmental repository. A small off-grid refrigerator for vaccines was also provided for occasions when there might be electrical outages, which were common in Third World countries.

Doctors Without Borders appealed to the two altruistic friends. Once the containers were packed and ready to go, they volunteered to oversee the delivery to a small hospital near the Pakistan/Afghanistan border that was in desperate need of the supplies.

# Chapter 46

Their journey to Peshawar and then on to the small rural Revenue Village where the Doctors Without Borders were working was arduous, depressing, and frightening. The women traveled along barely passable roads through a scarred landscape just to reach their destination. They thought they had their misgivings under control, but their driver picked up on their anxiety. As they unloaded the supplies and their few belongings, he warned, "Good luck ladies, you ain't seen nothing yet."

A young man wearing stained scrubs of indeterminate color greeted them, extending his hand to Marie. In broken English, he said, "Welcome, doctors. I know you must be tired. The trip is very difficult, but we are so glad you have come. I'm Pascal Benoit and I'm in charge of Camelot, in addition to being a surgeon."

Marie replied, "C'est agréable de vous rencontrer. Je peux parler avec vous en Français Si vous le souhaitez," letting him know she could speak with him in French if he wished. Pascal's appreciative smile indicated he approved of his new colleague.

"Between English and French, we will save the world," Pascal responded as he genially shook the hands of both doctors. Siobhan inwardly smiled at her friend's ability to reach out to people. She spoke all the romance languages fluently. With Slavic and Arabic, Marie was able to carry on basic communication. The same held true with many of the African languages. Her ability to assimilate a new language was uncanny.

Pascal brought them to their new quarters and then introduced them to the staff. When they opened containers of medical supplies, they were exuberant. The quality as well as the variety of these supplies far exceeded the haphazard disbursements they were used to receiving. And these supplies would be replenished as soon as a request was made, without them having to go through any red tape.

Marie and Siobhan remained in the small village for three difficult months. Every day brought misfortunes, both medically and emotionally. Living among people who were in constant danger of losing their land and/or their lives was an eye-opener, and the doctors learned that life in Third World countries often centers on pure survival rather than hope.

Siobhan was pleased that the work of Doctors Without Borders not only saved lives but also was emotionally uplifting for so many people. However, every day as she awoke she longed to return to Manhattan, finish her residency, and then return to her beloved Ireland, where she would launch her medical career.

Marie's response to this chaotic situation was typical of the way she dealt with life once she became a doctor. Everything centered on the present, and she gave little thought to the future. She had determined this tour was worthwhile; therefore, right now it was the core of her existence.

Within a short time, Marie had learned Pashto and some Punjabi, the languages of the area. The small town had once housed a music school, and the building was still intact. Although there was almost no furniture left inside, she was surprised to find a grand piano in fairly good condition.

An accomplished pianist, Marie shared her talent and brought joy to the young and old of the village with her mini-concerts. She learned and taught children's songs in Pashto, and every day she gave English lessons to anyone who was interested.

Siobhan had several nicknames for Marie. Sometimes she dubbed her Mother Theresa. At other times it would be Madame Curie, Alberta Einstein, Vanna Cliburn, or Martina Luther King. It seemed to Siobhan that Marie's capabilities were unlimited. But Marie dismissed Siobhan's pet names with a shrug. In spite of her talents, she was never self-serving.

When it was time for Marie and Siobhan to return to the States, the Taliban forces were closing in on areas nearby, so they needed to move quickly. Siobhan was packed and ready to leave while Marie was lagging behind, so Siobhan packed for her friend and then dragged her to the departing military transportation. News of Taliban atrocities had reached the doctors and aides, so many of them also piled onto the departing vehicles. Siobhan was relieved as the village faded into the distance, while Marie railed at leaving the residents to an inevitably cruel fate.

# Chapter 47

Returning to New York, Marie and Siobhan resumed their busy pediatric careers. Marie was in high demand and had several offers at other hospitals, but she remained at Mt. Carmel. Siobhan's desire to return to Ireland gathered momentum.

The two friends did manage to work in a trip to Galway, Ireland. They stayed in a tiny cottage facing the sea and visited Siobhan's family and friends. Marie fell in love with the Irish charm and could understand her friend's yearning to return to this captivating country.

When they got back to the States, Siobhan began to plan her move back to Ireland, while Marie became more and more concerned about the situation in Revenue Village. She heard from her Doctors Without Borders colleagues that the follow-up medical containers had not arrived. They did say, however, that the terrorists were concentrating on a large city much farther away so life was more stable in their area now.

Once again, Marie decided to deliver the containers to their destination, though Siobhan was not interested in making another trip. Within a week, the containers had been packed and Marie was on her way to Pakistan.

# Chapter 48

Five doctors drove forty kilometers to pick up Marie and the medical containers that had arrived in Peshawar. After giving Marie a warm welcome, Dr. Benoit told her that the group would be staying in Peshawar overnight. They planned to shop for supplies while they were there, as well as some items that might make life a bit more comfortable for their patients, such as blankets and bedding. Then he spoke with the station master and arranged for the medical containers to be stored at the station until the next morning.

Although the current atmosphere in Peshawar seemed almost normal, the 2014 school massacre that resulted in the deaths of one hundred thirty-two children and nine staff members remained in the back of everyone's mind. But the bustling market with its vibrant colors and tantalizing aromas was still a welcome reprieve from the dreariness of the small impoverished town where the doctors were working. They welcomed this brief interlude to indulge in simple activities that most people take for granted.

A Pakistani friend of Dr. Benoit owned a small apartment near the Meena Bazaar in Peshawar, and the doctors stayed there overnight. After dinner, they stayed up late talking about non-medical topics, something they rarely had the chance to do.

In the morning they drove to the shipping station to pick up the containers. They were halfway through loading their truck when the normal business chatter of people in the station changed abruptly to agitated shouting.

An agent darted toward them with bad news. Several bands of ISIL had joined forces, which gave them renewed strength. The rumor was they were descending on the outlying suburbs of Peshawar. Two small villages were said to have already fallen, though this had not yet been officially confirmed.

Dr. Benoit had to get back to Revenue Village to check on his colleagues and the defenseless people who lived there. But he had no idea if the village had been destroyed or bypassed by the terrorists. To go back in only one truck would be suicidal if terrorists were between Peshawar and their village, so Marie suggested they ask for an escort of Pakistani soldiers and then go back to the village with more vehicles in case they had to evacuate the residents.

All the doctors agreed on this strategy, but implementing it was not going to be easy. Luckily, the commander of the local army unit had family living in the village, so he ordered three army cargo vehicles to accompany the doctors' truck. Within a few hours the convoy was on its way, on the alert for trouble that could occur at any moment.

When they arrived at the village, an eerie silence coupled with the distinctive odor of nitroglycerin filled the air, which indicated there had been recent gunfire. The band slowly got out of their trucks, fearing an ambush. The village looked deserted, but after a few moments a doctor walked out of a partially destroyed building.

She showed no emotion as she walked, zombie-like, toward Dr. Benoit's vehicle. Marie took Jill's hand and pressed it to her heart. The doctor did not react to the contact. She was in a state of shock.

Were the terrorists still in the village? They needed to do something to help Jill back to reality, but they didn't have much time. Marie slapped Jill several times before she snapped out of her stupor. At first she didn't say a word, but as she remembered the horrors she had recently seen, she began to scream hysterically. The others were no closer to finding out what had happened than when she had been in her catatonic state.

Marie embraced the stricken woman, forming a cocoon of safety around her. For several minutes, she rocked Jill back and forth, back and forth. Slowly Jill came to grips with what had happened and realized that she needed to tell the others about it. Barely audible garbled words began to tumble out of her. Dr. Benoit, keeping his voice quiet and under control, asked Jill questions, repeating them several times until they got a coherent account of the attack.

Around 3 p.m., black-hooded terrorists stormed into Revenue Village, slaughtering anyone they came upon and then dragging the bodies into a wooden building far on the other side of town. After burning the building, they moved on. About two hundred lives were lost.

The death toll would have been larger, but some of the villagers were away when the ambush occurred. People from nearby villages had been providing essentials to those villages that had been hit by terrorists. The doctors from Revenue Village who hadn't gone with the group to pick up the medical containers, along with about twenty-five woman and ten children, had gone to a nearby town to deliver supplies.

As Jill finished her story, this other group was just returning home. Seeing the burned-out building, the women rushed to their homes, only to find them empty. Panicking, they ran back out to the trucks, screaming for their loved ones. Dr. Benoit explained as gently as he could what had happened to the other villagers. Overcome with emotion, the women clung to their remaining children and to each other, but not for long. Their grief had to be temporarily put on hold because all of the survivors were now in danger themselves.

The soldiers knew everyone would have to leave the village quickly, since terrorists often returned to previously sieged villages in order to pilfer buildings for useful items overlooked during the killing rampage. So they ordered everyone who had returned to the village to gather whatever essentials they could carry and then board the trucks.

# Chapter 49

Marie and seven of the children had been assigned to the last truck, along with several medical containers and boxes of canned food. After gathering a few items that would keep them warm on the ride to Peshawar, she and the children stopped briefly at the music building. She walked over to the piano and picked up her sheet music and then led the children out the door, where they were met by the sickening stench of burned wood and seared flesh.

As the children stood on the porch, Marie quickly double checked that they had what they needed. When the sun went down in that area, temperatures dropped dramatically, and it was already dark and chilly.

As Marie rummaged through a bag containing jackets, intent on what she was doing, one of the children yelled, "Dr. Marie, the truck is gone!"

That couldn't be! Marie was sure the child was mistaken. It was difficult to see in the darkness, and the truck might have moved to a different spot. Marie told the children to wait inside while she looked around, but she quickly realized that the truck had indeed left without them.

The communication between the four drivers had been minimal. The sounds of gunfire in the distance seemed to be coming closer, and they all knew an attack would come soon. They couldn't waste any time. Then the fourth driver saw the first three trucks pull away. He already had the medical containers and canned goods in the back of his truck and he didn't see anyone else in the village, so he followed the other trucks.

Marie and the children heard the gunfire too. There was no doubt it was getting closer. Marie struggled to stay calm. She had to do what she could to protect these children, even though at this moment she felt there was little hope that any of them would survive an attack.

She quickly looked around the music building. There really was no place to hide. And she didn't see anything that could be used as a weapon either.

Gathering the children and sitting them next to her right by the piano, Marie said, "Let's listen to music and play a game. Just keep looking at me. Listen to the beautiful music and follow my lead, no matter what happens around us. Do you think you can do that?"

The children nodded in agreement, and Marie began to play part of Rachmaninoff's Piano Concerto. The children loved this piece with its flamboyant beauty. Before she finished, it was obvious to Marie that there were others in the room, but for some reason they remained silent.

Marie ended that piece and quickly launched into some Pashto nursery rhymes, with the children singing, "cham cham cham, umbrella ley kar nikley hum, ghari aaiye phisley hum." This was a normal activity for them, since they sang nursery songs with the doctor every day. The uninvited "guests" listened, surprised to see them singing these traditional childhood songs without fear, in spite of what was going on around them.

And then suddenly the earth began to rumble. Speaking to the children in English, Marie told them to keep singing. She could hear whispering among the intruders, who weren't sure what to do.

# NICHOLAS

# Chapter 50

Matthew understood that Siobhan's concern about Marie precluded any thought of finalizing their wedding plans. Her best friend could well be dead or dying. As he tenderly cradled Siobhan in his arms, the sorrow was almost too much to bear.

Nicholas felt sorry for everything the couple was going through. At the same time, he was inwardly furious at this Marie, whom he had never met, for being the cause of all this turmoil. He couldn't understand why she would put herself in such danger in an unstable Third World country.

Nicholas used his money and influence to consult with those in touch with that part of the world. Tonight he'd gotten word that there had been a massacre at Revenue Village. The most disturbing piece of news was that the rescue trucks had returned without Marie and seven of the children. And it was too dangerous for the trucks to go back now.

Nicholas heard the latest news around 11 p.m. and was at a loss as to how he would relay the information to his friends. Why was this his responsibility? He didn't even know that idiot of a woman whose misguided altruism threatened to ruin the lives of his closest friends.

The next morning when Claire arrived at work, she found Nicholas in the same chair he had been sitting in when he'd received the devastating news.

.

# MARIE

# Chapter 51

Marie's gaze never wavered from the sheet of music, but the nearness of evil filled her with dread. She couldn't believe the children were still following her directions. They kept their eyes only on her, acting as if everything were normal and they were having one of their daily lessons. She hoped and prayed that the children would be spared a torturous death, but she saw no way out of their predicament.

"Keep playing," one of the intruders commanded in English. "Don't stop for a moment."

Marie switched to a piece from "Carnival of the Animals," a favorite of the children. They responded by clapping.

Now the speaker spoke in Pashto, making it evident that he was not speaking to her. He didn't know that she understood every word he said or that she also recognized his voice.

He obviously was someone in authority. He told the others that the whole world seemed to know what was going on in this village and that his orders were to bring the captives to a command post where they could be used for prisoner exchanges. Then he dismissed the other men.

Once the footsteps had drifted away, Marie uttered her first word, "Paul."

"Yes, Marie."

Paul had been a medical student interning at the same hospital as Marie and Siobhan, and the three had become good friends. At first Paul was likeable, with a great sense of humor and an easygoing attitude. Then his mood began to change. He didn't laugh much anymore, and eventually he stopped hanging out with his friends. After several unsuccessful attempts to reach out to Paul, the rest of his friends finally gave up and left him alone. A few months later, he left the hospital abruptly and disappeared.

Paul directed everyone to get into his vehicle. Marie sat next to him as they left the village, wondering what the future would hold for her and these children. The trip seemed endless. Paul barely uttered a word. The children never muttered a complaint, even though they were cold and uncomfortable.

Eventually the blackness of night gave way to the first inkling of dawn. Marie thought she could make out an outline of something in the distance. After a few minutes, she realized the outline was a city miles away from them.

Abruptly the vehicle stopped. "This is as far as I can go. You must get out."

"Where are we?" Marie asked.

"Peshawar."

Peshawar might mean safety, but Marie figured it had to be miles away.

"Get out now."

The young captives stumbled out of the vehicle, some just waking up. The mountainous Pakistani air was bitter cold at dawn. Marie carried the youngest, a three year old. The oldest, whose eleventh birthday had coincided with the massacre, lifted a tiny five-year-old girl to his shoulders, where she immediately fell asleep. And so the little group began their trek toward Peshawar.

Marie feared Peshawar was beyond their grasp, but surrendering to hopelessness was not an option. Music had charged their spirits before and she felt that it would again. This time she chose a frivolous American folk tune that was a reverse counting song.

As Marie began to sing, the children joined in:

"Ninety-nine bottles of beer on the wall,
Ninety-nine bottles of beer.

If one of those bottles should happen to fall,
Ninety-eight bottles of beer on the wall."

The singing gave them a respite from despair, and weak laughter erupted when they started to mix up the numbers. But soon even this diversion was beginning to wear thin. Marie was desperately trying to think of another activity to engage the children when she thought she saw something on the bleak, treeless road ahead.

Almost imperceptible at first, the vision turned into a cavalcade of moving wheels.

Marie wondered, *Could it be the trucks returning for us?*

The caravan stopped about forty feet ahead of them. A Pakistani soldier stepped out of the first truck and began calling to her. At first the words were inaudible, but after many repetitions Marie realized he was shouting "Doctor, Doctor Eagan."

Before she could even respond, a truck door opened and about twenty people came rushing toward her and the children. At the halfway point, loved ones recognized each other. Mothers ran even more quickly to embrace their children. The women who lost their husbands during the massacre had not lost everything after all. Because of Marie, their children's lives had been saved.

Marie related to the authorities that an unknown ISIL soldier had driven them from Revenue Village and dropped them off about a mile back. She did not mention Paul's name. No matter what he had done before, he had saved their lives.

Finally, Marie was only responsible for herself. That evening she sank into a deep sleep that relieved her from the responsibility she had felt for the lives of seven other human beings.

Marie was in a daze while other people made plans for her return home, but brief glimpses of reality worked their way into her hazy consciousness. She remembered talking to Siobhan on the phone and something about a wedding; she also remembered saying goodbye to the people of Revenue Village and later boarding a plane. Then sleep once again engulfed her, until she fully woke up in a hospital room in Germany, where she was being monitored until doctors felt she was ready for the trip back to the States.

PJ Dischino

# NICHOLAS

# Chapter 52

It was still early when Claire got off the elevator and opened the door to Garlow and Associates. As she went into her own office, she noticed that Nicholas' door was slightly ajar, which was odd. He wasn't usually in the office before 9 a.m.

Claire's phone started to ring, but she ignored it. Instead, she switched direction and headed toward the open door. Nicholas was sitting in an awkward position at his desk, cradling his head with his arms. He didn't stir until Claire gave him a gentle nudge.

"Why didn't you sleep on the couch if you spent the night here?" she asked.

"I got some really disturbing news around 11 p.m. last night, and I've been sitting here in a stupor ever since. Terrorists attacked the village where Siobhan's friend, Marie, was working with Doctors Without Borders. There are reports of a massacre. Some villagers were rescued after an initial attack, but Marie and seven children were left behind. There is no way they could have survived a second attack by the terrorists.

"The last message I got before I nodded off was that a bomb or fire had destroyed the village. I'm not quite sure. Claire, I dread having to tell Siobhan and Matthew about this."

This news made Claire heartsick. She too dreaded having to give her son and future daughter-in-law such tragic news.

Claire's phone was ringing again. Her assistant had just come in. She threw her purse on her desk and rushed to pick up the call. A moment later, she burst into Nicholas' office, announcing, "Claire, there's a very important call that you need to take. Someone who has important information about Dr. Eagan has been trying to get ahold of you."

"Sorry, we were distracted. I'll take the call now," Claire replied. As she hurried back to her own office, Nicholas' phone started ringing too.

This morning's messages brought much better news. Amazingly, Marie and the seven children had been rescued. They were all OK. Claire immediately called Siobhan, whose reaction was unintelligible but jubilant.

Several hours later, Siobhan was able to connect with Marie. She was bubbling over with happiness that her best friend was alive and could be her maid of honor. She was overjoyed that she would be reunited with Marie soon.

As Nicholas' euphoria subsided, he realized he was still angry—angry at a woman he'd never met who had upset the lives of people he cared about deeply. He would help Marie get home as quickly and comfortably as possible, but after that he hoped their encounters would be limited.

# Chapter 53

Marie was more than happy to let her friend plan her trip home. Siobhan, in high spirits once again, laid out plans for her friend's return and also picked up with her wedding arrangements. Now she could finally set a date.

Once Marie had arrived in Germany, Siobhan talked with her every day, filling her friend in on Matthew and his family. She also told Marie about Nicholas, not only because he was making it possible for Matthew and her to live in Ireland but also because he had played a role in getting Marie out of Pakistan. Much as Marie loved Siobhan, she still found it hard to concentrate on so much news all at once, and so the details became a blur.

On the fifth day after the massacre, Marie left the German hospital. An anonymous benefactor had arranged for a smart new wardrobe of casual clothes and matching accessories to be delivered to the hospital the previous day. And just that morning, a hair stylist had arrived to give her a chic new hairdo. Grateful to trade hospital gowns and the outfit she had been wearing throughout her ordeal for something more stylish, Marie prepared for her trip. However, she was determined to return all but the outfit she was wearing home to the sender, as well as pay for everything else. Of course, first she would have to find out who this mysterious benefactor was!

But there were still a few more surprises. At 11 a.m., a limo picked her up at the hospital and drove her to the airport, where she boarded a private jet.

Marie contentedly drifted in and out of sleep on the flight to New York. A few minutes after the plane landed, Siobhan rushed to greet her, with tears streaming down her face. Once the two friends had regained their composure, Marie noticed six complete strangers beaming at her. Siobhan introduced her fiancé, Matthew; Claire and Henry; and Kimberly, Jason, and Diane, who was sitting in her stroller playing with a puzzle.

These strangers enveloped her in warmth, simply because of their fondness for Siobhan. Only a few days ago Marie had been prepared to face death, and now she was filled with gratitude for the concern and caring being showered upon her by her old friend as well as a whole new group of friends.

After collecting Marie's belongings, Siobhan grasped Marie's arm and led her to the car. On the way, she explained that they were all going to have dinner at one of the best hotels in New York. She and Marie would stay there overnight, and Siobhan's family would arrive the next day. They would be on holiday for the next two weeks, culminating in the wedding of Siobhan and Matthew.

In an intimate private room of a posh hotel in Manhattan, seven adults and a precious little girl shared a meal. In the midst of elegant surroundings and warm companionship, Marie finally let herself relax, putting aside for now the horrors of her recent experience.

Shortly after they finished their meal, Kimberly's daughter announced, "I want to go home now. Good night, nice lady."

After the laughter subsided, Kimberly added, "Diane isn't very subtle but she's right. It's time for all of us to say goodnight to this 'nice lady.' I know I speak for everyone when I say we are so happy you are safe. You are everything Siobhan described and more."

Matthew chimed in, declaring, "And now let the wedding plans proceed!"

Before everyone went their separate ways, Marie said, "I'm really grateful for everything you've all done for me, but I have to ask who my secret benefactor is. First, some private company aided my rescue. Then I was flown to a top-notch hospital in Germany, where I stayed in a private room for four days and had a whole new wardrobe delivered to me. Then I was taken by limo to the airport, where I boarded a private plane. Siobhan, the last time I saw you, you were planning to go home to Ireland to practice. Now you are getting married. Matthew, are you my benefactor?"

No one replied immediately. Matthew finally responded, "No Marie, I'm definitely not in a position to make all of that happen, but I have to say I have never met anyone more deserving of special treatment than you. Siobhan will fill you in later tonight."

With that, everyone gave Marie a hug and said goodnight. As soon as they were gone, Siobhan led an even more bewildered Marie to a sumptuous suite in the same hotel.

# Chapter 54

It was not easy to bring a yawning Marie up-to-date at 1 a.m. in the morning, but Siobhan finally felt her dearest friend understood that the wedding was in two weeks and that she would be the maid of honor. However, by the time she got to the details of the secret benefactor, Marie was fast asleep.

Marie woke up to surroundings befitting royalty. The furnishings and view were grand, and her closet was brimming with coordinated ensembles for any occasion. She found the opulence to be overwhelming. Once again, she resolved to wear as few of the clothes as possible and to return everything else.

The days before the wedding passed quickly. Marie felt as if someone was holding a remote control and playing her life on fast forward as the parties, fittings, and gatherings whizzed by.

Siobhan's family included her mother, dad, and four siblings, her grandmother, and three aunts. Spending time with them was a high note for Marie, since she had met these endearing relatives when she had traveled to Ireland with Siobhan.

The two young women had stayed in a tiny cottage almost touching the sea. Every morning a wonderful lady delivered a warm Irish breakfast complete with the most mouth-watering scones lathered with fresh butter. The days there passed quickly as they soaked up the sea air and local hospitality. Her time in Ireland was one of Marie's fondest memories.

Two days after her arrival in New York, Marie finally got to meet her benefactor, Nicholas Garlow. It was at a luncheon held at the Garlow offices. Elegantly appointed tables filled a corner room with a magnificent view of Manhattan on two sides. The gathered guests chattered amiably until the door opened.

All talking ceased. Everyone held their breath, as if American royalty was about to enter the room. A moment later a tall blond man in his early thirties walked in, wearing a bright smile that immediately put everyone at ease.

Nicholas welcomed the Irish clan with warm humor but never acknowledged Marie. While Marie took no notice of the slight, Siobhan and Matthew's family were silently appalled.

Claire muttered under her breath, "What the hell?" Marie couldn't figure out why she was so upset.

Meanwhile, Nicholas gave his attention to an attractive brunette who gazed at him adoringly.

Claire muttered again, complaining that Nicholas hadn't told her he was inviting anyone. Claire had made the seating arrangements, placing Marie next to Nicholas because of all the effort he had made to save Marie and bring her home. Marie, who didn't know that Nicholas was her secret benefactor, was confused.

Claire firmly grabbed Marie's wrist and led her directly to Nicholas, who made it a point to introduce his latest companion, Liz, in a most audible voice. Claire didn't even acknowledge her. Instead, she announced, "Mr. Garlow, this is Dr. Marie Eagan, the brave lady you helped to rescue."

Marie moved forward, anxious to thank Mr. Garlow for all he had done. She smiled at her benefactor, but quickly noticed that his expression had changed. He gazed at her as if she were an intruder. Marie felt snubbed, but he had done so much for her that she had to respond to Claire's introduction.

"Mr. Garlow, I thought you would arrive riding a white horse. You certainly are my hero. Thank you for all you have done."

Sensing that she was annoying Nicholas, Marie stepped back quickly. She resolved to keep her distance, especially after hearing his clipped response, "It was nothing."

Marie turned away from the rude and unpleasant man and walked over to talk with Siobhan's mother. "I certainly didn't win Brownie points with our host!"

Shocked, Mrs. Innes asked, "Why would he be rude to you when he is so pleasant and kind to everyone else?"

Marie shrugged her shoulders and declared that she was completely in the dark. Just then she noticed that Claire was pulling Nicholas aside and that her expression was quite stern as she spoke to him.

Nicholas' surly behavior toward Marie did not abate one bit after his brief conversation with Claire, but it lost some of its impact a few days before the wedding when Dr. Pascal Benoit arrived in New York. The following Tuesday, he was to appear before the National Committee of American Affairs in Washington, D.C., to testify about the horrific conditions Doctors Without Borders were experiencing in Pakistan. As soon as Siobhan found out he was going to be in the States, she invited him to her wedding.

This couldn't have worked out more advantageously for Marie. Often the best man and the maid of honor spend some time together during the wedding festivities, but Nicholas purposely avoided Marie. When Dr. Benoit noticed how aloof Nicholas was to her, Marie told him what had happened the night she met him. Pascal couldn't believe that someone who had gone out of his way to help Marie get back to the States would treat her so badly when he actually met her. And so Pascal became Marie's ardent companion during the wedding festivities. For some strange reason, this infuriated Nicholas.

The wedding took place in a large ballroom of the same hotel. It was amazing how quickly the day went, given all the months of planning that had gone into the preparations. Suddenly the celebration was ending. Her best friend threw her bouquet directly at Marie, who had no choice but to catch it. The bride and groom left on their honeymoon as the guests danced a few more dances.

Claire was torn between conflicting emotions. She was overflowing with joy at her son's choice of a wife and their perfect wedding. But she was also very angry with Nicholas and felt the need to tell him how she felt.

As Marie hands grasped the wedding bouquet, Claire walked over to Nicholas, who was standing on the sidelines with his date. She briskly tapped his shoulder to get his attention and asked him if they could speak somewhere alone.

Nicholas noticed her stern expression, which made him feel like a child about to be reprimanded. He suspected that his churlish behavior toward Marie was behind her request.

"Of course," he responded, leading Claire to the nearest empty room, which turned out to be a utility room.

Claire burst into her tirade immediately: "It was you who helped save Marie's life, provided her with the best of medical care, bought her a new wardrobe, and then even flew her home on your private jet, so how could you treat her so shabbily when you met her in person? Your insolence is inexcusable. The entire wedding party was embarrassed, except for you.

"Everyone else admired her as soon as they met her. She is sweet, intelligent, generous, thoughtful, gracious, and brave…." Claire stumbled, trying to think of more complementary adjectives to describe Marie. Finally, she just decided to move on. "You are brilliant when it comes to sizing up people you encounter in your everyday business dealings. No one comes close to matching your architectural talent, your creative ideas, and your business acumen. You are a genius—with one glaring exception. When it comes to personal relations, you are totally inept!"

Nicholas listened to Claire's diatribe. He knew she cared deeply about him or this conversation would never be taking place. Nevertheless, the protective defense he had spent decades perfecting was now under attack, and that made him bristle.

"Nicholas, you endured an unhappy childhood. That has made it difficult for you to open up about your past, to trust people, to find love. Look at your three failed engagements. You picked three women who weren't right for you, and when they inevitably did little things that bothered you, you blew those things out of proportion and used them as an excuse to get out of the relationships."

Claire searched for the right words to reach Nicholas. "You have no family. You are all alone. And I suspect your distress rears its ugly head whenever you have to attend family functions where you feel you are the outsider. And so you act obnoxiously and push people away when what you want most is to feel connected to them.

"I'm not saying that Marie is necessarily the one for you, although you do have a great deal in common. You both had childhoods from hell and you are both still alone, even though you have some good friends. So what I AM saying is that I really think you are missing out on connecting with someone extraordinary by keeping Marie at arm's length. I have only known her for a few days, and I can see what a remarkable person she is.

"I also noticed you watching Marie and Dr. Benoit. You looked angry, but I think you were really jealous. Siobhan mentioned that Marie felt hurt when you snubbed her, but she made sure to have a good time in spite of your rejection. Your attitude confused her, but she tried to move past it. She didn't want her best friend's wedding to be ruined because the best man couldn't even be civil to her.

"I probably have no right to interfere with your private life, but your actions really upset me. And I'm not the only one who is appalled by your behavior."

Claire stood looking at him for a few seconds before she added, "And you have been absolutely horrible to Jennifer, who is almost certainly your sister. She worried about her baby brother and searched for him for years, yet when she thought she had found him, you refused to answer any personal questions and tossed her aside, demanding that she stay out of your life. You hurt Jennifer terribly, but I suspect that in pushing her away you hurt yourself even more."

Claire's expression softened once she had released her bottled up concerns. She dearly loved Nicholas, and the way he avoided his emotional problems saddened her.

It was Nicholas who broke the silence. "I could fire you for what you just said to me, but then there would be severance to pay. And I would have to break in a new CFO and find a new life manager and best friend. That would take years."

His penetrating green eyes revealed his deep affection for this woman who had so suddenly revealed the defenses that kept him "safe" and yet blocked his ability to be vulnerable and honest with women. Smiling, he reached over to the woman who had exposed his personal demons and hugged her tenderly.

"Why haven't you ever mentioned all this before?"

"I was waiting for the right moment, and I guess this was finally it."

"It will take me awhile to digest what you just dumped on me."

As Claire opened the door to leave, she warned, "Don't wait too long."

# Chapter 55

After the guests were gone, Marie and Siobhan's parents sat downstairs in the corner of the lobby. It was after 11:00, and they had that let down feeling that comes over people when an important day has ended.

Marie suddenly felt terribly alone, yet she tried to keep the conversation light. She mentioned that she was going to stay at Siobhan's old apartment for a short time until she decided what she wanted to do next. But tomorrow she planned to visit with her friend, Ben.

Claire and her family found the little group in the lobby and joined them for a few minutes. They talked about the beautiful wedding and how much they had enjoyed meeting each other. The Inneses mentioned that they were staying in New York for three more days before returning to Ireland, and Claire suggested they all meet again for one last dinner while they were still in New York.

Before they left, Kimberly gave Marie a hug and whispered that her mother had confronted Nicholas about his obnoxious behavior. Marie's heart sank. She certainly didn't want Claire to get in trouble on her account.

After the Talmadge family was gone, the Inneses laughed about how they would miss the amenities of the huge hotel. Margot Innes joked that she had forgotten how to cook, and her husband gave her a look of mock panic. For her part, Marie couldn't get out of the place fast enough.

As the Inneses got up and walked toward the elevator, they asked Marie if she was ready to go upstairs. "I think I'll stay here awhile longer. I have so much to think about."

"You're coming to Ireland in two weeks when Siobhan and Matthew are there, aren't you?"

"I don't know, Margot. I need to figure out what the future holds for me."

"We won't take that as an answer. The future can wait for a few more weeks!"

They got into the elevator and Marie felt lonelier than ever. Nicholas' behavior disheartened her, although she didn't know why it should bother her. Having avoided romantic encounters as a result of her lonely upbringing, she didn't realize that she was actually attracted to the man who was causing her such distress.

She dozed off briefly but was suddenly awakened by a commotion being made by a couple getting off the elevator. It took a few seconds before she realized it was Nicholas and his date, who had had a bit too much to drink. He was trying to steer her toward the exit amidst a barrage of barbed expletives she was directing at him. Just before they got to the door, she slapped his face. Whatever happened outside was quick, since Nicholas returned within a few minutes. Marie stood up to leave, as she wanted to avoid any encounter with him.

When Nicholas saw her, he walked directly over to her and stopped right in front of her, leaving almost no space between them.

"So, am I being evicted from the hotel now that the wedding is over?" she asked.

A broad smile suddenly lit up his serious face, exposing an attractive dimple. His deep ocean green eyes danced in response to the beautiful face before him. He didn't know what was happening. He certainly wasn't naïve about sexual attraction, but this feeling was something he had never experienced before.

"I'm a fool, Marie. I've been acting like an ass and I need to apologize to you."

"Yes you do, but at this point I really don't care. I've enjoyed myself in spite of your rude behavior."

The banter went back and forth for a few minutes before the two settled into a more serious conversation. They spent the rest of the night together talking about their hopes and fears, sharing their dreams as well as their nightmares. By dawn they both knew they had finally found what had been missing in their lives—true love. Hand in hand, they walked slowly through the lobby and took the elevator up to Nicholas' penthouse.

# Chapter 56

Never once in his life had Nicholas felt a passionate yet bonding type of love. His sex life had been physically satisfying but emotionally sterile. Cupid had never found his mark. As each of his wedding dates approached, Nicholas had pulled back from making a permanent commitment. His would-be mates and their families suddenly became overbearing and loathsome in his mind. All he knew was that he'd always wanted out. "Unlucky in love" became his personal mantra.

Suddenly the worlds of both Nicholas and Marie changed; most importantly, their lives merged. For the rest of the weekend, the two spoke in more depth about their life experiences. Marie described the horrors she had faced that still haunted her. Nicholas talked about his childhood insecurities that had followed him into adulthood and revealed the guilt he felt for the way he had treated his sister. Now was the time to rectify his blunder.

They both decided to prepare for a life together by tying up their loose ends. On Monday morning, they agreed to split up for the day so that each of them could do what they needed to do and then meet at Nicholas' apartment at 5 p.m. There was no time to see Ben and Jan that day, but they would arrange that for tomorrow.

Before they went their own ways for the day, Marie said emphatically that she wanted no part of Nicholas' vast empire and suggested they draw up a prenuptial agreement to preserve his fortune. A roll of his eyes accompanied by an annoyed expression convinced Marie to drop the subject temporarily.

When Nicholas walked into Claire's office with a beaming grin on his boyish face, she was confused. This was hardly what she had expected after her last conversation with him. Approaching Claire, he placed an envelope on her desk.

"Good morning, Mr. Garlow. You certainly are in a good mood. It's wonderful to see you so upbeat. Quite a change, I must say." Picking up the envelope she inquired, "Is this something that I need to take care of right away?"

"Claire, this is a very small way to thank you for changing the course of my life. You are the reason I am the happiest man on this planet– no, I'll go so far as to extend my jubilation to the farthest galaxy! Open the envelope."

Bewildered, Claire flipped open the barely sealed flap of the envelope. Inside was a detailed two-week itinerary in Ireland for ten people, the date to be determined.

"Nicholas, this is totally unnecessary. If you are happy, then I am happy! Actually, the entire company is happy. You have been, shall I say, a bit crusty lately."

Nicholas interrupted. "There's a motive behind my gift besides wanting to acknowledge that you did absolutely the right thing when you confronted me. I guess my background caused me to fight the one thing that I needed–someone to love."

"I assume you are speaking of Marie. I couldn't be happier!"

"The wedding will be in Ireland."

Giving Nicholas a warm hug, Claire exclaimed, "Let me call her right this minute!"

"That's not a good idea right now. I haven't asked her yet."

"Nicholas, you're making all these plans and she hasn't said yes?"

"Don't worry. All you need to know is she loves me and I love her. Here's my plan. By 4:30 this afternoon I want to have a party set up in our banquet room, the room where we held Matthew and Siobhan's gathering. Invite everyone who's at the office today.

"I'm going to talk to Brian and will be back in an hour. First, I need to look over the calendar to arrange dates."

Claire thought this was rather presumptive since Marie's "yes" was not official but decided to stifle her thoughts and go with the flow.

"It is now 8:45. Do you think you can pull it together in time?"

"I'm on it!" Claire replied as she picked up the phone to call the caterer she had used for Matthew's wedding, as well as all of their important business events. She knew they wouldn't let a tight time frame hamper a request from their top client.

With an impish grin, Nicholas rushed out the door. Sliding into the back seat of his waiting limo, he directed his driver to the same jeweler he'd used for his three previous engagements.

# Chapter 57

Cal Reston pushed open his front door after a week-long business trip. Being away held no pleasure for him. He couldn't wait to be home with his precious Jenny, two-year-old Craig, and new baby daughter, Dana.

Jenny was holding Dana and Craig was dragging his favorite pull toy around the family room when they heard Cal's suitcase drop on the foyer floor.

"Daddy's home!" Jenny announced, and they rushed to bombard Cal with hugs and kisses. In the middle of their little reunion, the phone rang. Cal sighed and picked up the receiver.

"Hello, this is Cal Reston. May I help you?"

"Hi Cal. This is Nicholas Garlow. I know you have no desire to hear my voice, but I would like to talk to Jennifer."

Cal walked toward his office, telling Jenny that he needed to get the caller some information.

"You are quite right, Nicholas. We have no desire to talk to you or ever see you again. You have no idea how much you hurt my wife. She searched for years, longing for her baby brother who had disappeared. When she thought there was a possibility it might be you, she was ecstatic. You literally broke her heart, so I would prefer we have no further contact with you."

"Cal, you couldn't be more justified in your anger. I am not going to use my background as an excuse. Something recently happened that finally made me see how I've hurt people just to protect myself from my past. You might think people can't change, but I want to show you that I can. I don't want to interfere with your lives, but I do want to tell Jennifer how much I regret my behavior. I went through hell as a child and so did she. I should have been sensitive to her pain."

"Nicholas, although it is against my better judgment, it's Jennifer's decision. Will you hold on? I'll tell her you're on the line. Then we'll take it from there."

Cal found Jenny changing baby Dana. He reported what Nicholas had said, trying to keep a neutral expression on his face.

When Jenny asked him for advice, he replied, "Honey, this is strictly your decision. I don't want you ever to regret anything because of something I might say."

"Cal, if he upsets me, I *will* hang up on him."

"Just know I support you, whatever you decide to do."

Jennifer apprehensively picked up the phone. Nicholas began by asking about her family. It was the type of discussion one would have with a dear friend, which threw her off balance. She expected to be angry, but his voice had a calming effect on her.

Cal referred to his childhood as one reason for the protective armor he had been wearing to guard himself from disappointment, as well as torment. But that armor had made it impossible for him to get close to anyone—until Claire had confronted him. Her intervention had been a revelation. It amazed him how blind he had been.

Marie was next on his list. He talked about her with such love and joy that Jennifer's years of heartache began to melt away. She interrupted to tell him how happy she was for him.

"It's so sad that we were separated when I was so young. I missed out on so much by not having a loving family. I'm so sorry for any pain I've caused you, Jennifer, and I'd like to make a whole new start for us. I hope Cal will be OK with it. I know how he feels. I never was in love before, but now I would go to any length to protect Marie."

Nicholas went on to describe the party at which he planned to propose to Marie. He hoped Jenny and her family would be part of the special celebration. He suggested she talk it over with Cal and get back to him.

Jennifer described the conversation in detail as Cal listened, his emotions tangled with what he felt was right and how Jennifer felt. Jennifer mentioned that they were to act as if the party was solely a reunion between brother and sister until the engagement was announced. Her brother's last words before they ended the conversation were that the occasion truly was a double celebration.

As she described the conversation, Jenny sounded upbeat and excited again, something Cal could not easily dismiss. If it were up to him, the name Nicholas would never be mentioned again, but he could tell that Jenny wanted and needed to go to the party. The sadness that comes from years of heartbreak might never heal completely, but a new beginning softens the pain.

Six hours later the four Restons got into the limo Nicholas sent to pick them up.

# Chapter 58

Actually, it was over two hours before Nicholas got back to Claire. Both of them had been able to cross off several "to do" items during that time. Nicholas filled Claire in about Jennifer and told her to plan for four more people at the celebration. Claire had already contacted everyone else on the invitation list and had also taken care of not only the caterer but the florist as well.

Marie was not privy to any of this. She had been busy packing up her belongings that she had kept at Siobhan's apartment while she had been away. Around 1 p. m. Nicholas called and filled her in about his conversation with Jenny. He explained that he was having a formal get together at his office around 5:30 for his reunion with his sister. Marie was thrilled that Nicholas had taken this giant step.

"I have to leave now. Go to Fabian's for a dress. If you have any questions, call Claire."

The conversation was over before she could question why this all had to take place in one day. The doorbell rang. It was Nicholas' driver ready to take her to Fabian's.

Fabian's head designer and coordinator brought out ten "appropriate" cocktail dresses for Marie's perusal. But "appropriate" was far from what Marie had in mind. This was a party for Nicholas to erase past mistakes and embrace his sister with the love she deserved. This was not a red carpet affair. The dresses fell short of their purpose. She was wasting her time at Fabian's.

In Marie's college days she had done some modeling, and she usually worked for one particular agency. They loved using her for a variety of reasons. A knock-out-gorgeous model is quite unique, and Marie also conveyed an intriguing message when photographed.

Paine, the manager in charge of selecting the models' outfits for the shows, adored Marie. He had often told her that if she ever needed a designer outfit she should just come to him. Favored models often could choose past season outfits. Marie had never taken advantage of this; but after a short time at Fabians, she decided to take Paine up on his offer.

At the agency, she spotted the perfect dress. Although the off-white fabric appeared almost fragile, the flowing skirt radiated a luxurious elegance. Tiny pleats covered the bodice. The thin straps and narrow cummerbund fashioned in a deep magenta made the dress absolutely stunning. Paine brought over a pair of Jimmy Choo glimmer cut-out shoes that reminded her of glass slippers. A tiny antique sequined purse completed the effect.

At 5:15 Claire and Kimberly picked Marie up at her hotel room, explaining that Nicholas was running late. Marie felt relieved to see their elegant outfits, thankful that she was not over-dressed.

Entering the banquet room, Marie caught her breath. The decorations were classic and softly elegant, with a Garden Party theme. In the middle of the room, a miniature English garden surrounded a rippling water fountain and featured moss roses intertwined with lupine and phlox in hues of dusty rose and white. At the surrounding tables, crystal vases filled with pink cosmos and blue larkspur popped against the crisp white table linens and complemented the gray and pink floral china.

Over champagne and caviar Marie and Jenny marveled that Claire and Nicholas had been able to pull this all together in just one day. Marie told Jenny how happy Nicholas was to be reunited with her. Jenny smiled to herself, knowing that the real guest of honor had no inkling that this was really all for her.

After half an hour the guests sat down at their assigned tables and dined on their choice of English rib roast with Yorkshire pudding or Irish salmon with dill sauce, followed by English Trifle for dessert.

As flutes of champagne were being filled by the wait staff, Nicholas stood up and called for everyone's attention. After explaining a bit about his family history and his separation from his sister when he was a baby, he shared his joy at being reunited with her.

Introducing Jenny and her family, Nicholas declared, "So much time has been lost, but that doesn't matter. Right now I am fortunate to have a sister, a brother-in-law, a nephew, and a brand new niece."

As the guests began to raise their glasses, Nicholas added, "Hold on. I'm not quite finished."

Turning to Marie, he told his guests about the wonderful woman he had recently met, noting that it had taken him three previous tries before he got it right. He spoke of how close he had come to messing things up with Marie due to his own insecurities, and how his good friend Claire had helped him realize that he had been running away from what he wanted most—true love. To share the rest of his life with this incredible woman was truly his heart's desire.

Then he tenderly took Marie's hand. As he pulled a small box out of his pocket and handed it to her, he asked her if she would marry him. The contents of the box could only be a ring, but Nicholas explained that Marie disliked ostentation and so he tried to select a ring that would fall in line with her own style.

Marie managed to mumble "yes, oh yes" as Nicholas handed her the box. Guests thought it a bit odd. Didn't the perspective fiancé place the ring on his beloved's finger?

In a state of shock, Marie struggled to open the box. Her fingers just didn't want to move properly. Finally she got the ribbon untied. Inside the outer box she found a cheap cardboard container rather than a typical ring box.

As she removed the top, Marie stared at its contents for what seemed a full minute to the onlookers. *Where's the ring?* they wondered. *How many carats is it?*

Finally, Marie began to laugh as if someone had just told her the funniest joke. As she pulled the contents out of its box, the bewildered guests were shocked to see a huge plastic "stone" in a ring like a child might win as a party prize. As she gleefully modeled her magnificent "rock" for the guests, they got the joke and started to laugh with her.

A short time later, Nicholas led Marie into a small room where a jeweler displayed a variety of elegant rings in a black velvet case. After spending twenty minutes trying on one gorgeous ring after another, Marie zeroed in on a princess cut yellow diamond surrounded by smaller baguettes and set in platinum. What determined her choice was its simplicity, the delicacy of the color, and the beautiful mounting.

Marie didn't realize that while it wasn't the largest of the stones set before her, it was quite rare, which actually made it the most valuable ring on display. If she had known how expensive it was, she never would have chosen that particular ring. But at least for the moment, the jeweler and Nicholas were the only ones aware of the ring's value.

PJ Dischino

# LILY,
# MARIE,
# NICHOLAS

# Chapter 59

A new day brought forth a sense of joy that neither Marie nor Nicholas had known before. Marie remembered that she wanted to see Ben and his new love, Jan. And now she had some wonderful news to share with him too!

Ben answered on the first ring. His caring voice always managed to warm her entire being. There was so much news for both of them to share. Ben suggested that the two couples get together that night to celebrate, and they arranged to meet for dinner at 7 p.m.

After a marvelous evening, the group said good-bye around 10 p.m. An hour later, Marie's cell phone rang.

"Marie, I'm so sorry to bother you, but something terrible has happened to Lily. We're on the way to the hospital now," Ben said anxiously.

"Are you going to Mt. Carmel?"

"Yes. We should be there in about fifteen minutes."

"We're on our way too."

Marie yanked open the doors of the familiar Emergency Wing and immediately inquired about Lily. The Emergency Room doctor said that Lily was about to go into surgery, explaining that a large piece of glass had penetrated the child's upper arm. She had lost a lot of blood, probably caused by a severed artery.

Similar injuries were quite familiar to those who served with Doctors Without Borders. Marie consulted with the surgeon and suggested a procedure that combat doctors had been using successfully. The technique stopped the bleeding, and a blood transfusion helped to get Lily stabilized. Slowly her color, blood pressure, and all her vitals returned to normal. Since an X-ray revealed no artery was severed, the doctors stitched her wounds and then moved Lily into a room.

Sitting next to the little girl's bed, Marie softly called Lily's name. Slowly the child opened her eyes and immediately recognized the doctor who had taken care of her before.

"Where's Ben?' she asked in a tiny, frail voice.

"He's right outside. He will be so happy to know you are all right."

"Is Carla dead?"

Marie had no idea who Lily was talking about until a nurse explained that an older girl who had been found with Lily was still in surgery. Marie promised Lily that she would find out how Carla was doing.

Marie rushed to find Ben, who was in the waiting room with Jan, Nicholas, and Mrs. Andrews. The ashen look on the manager's face was an indication of the agony she had been going through due to guilt as well as a sincere concern for Lily's well-being.

After updating everyone on Lily's condition, Marie excused herself to find out about Carla. By this time, Carla was in the Recovery Room, but there was no one waiting to find out if she was going to be OK. She didn't have anyone who cared about her.

A policeman sat in a chair in the hall waiting to question her. He told Marie that Carla was a foster child who had attacked her foster father with a piece of glass from a broken mirror. The man was in surgery right now, and doctors weren't sure he was going to make it through the night.

According to the wife, she heard screams upstairs and when she came into Carla's room, she found her bloodied husband slumped on the floor amid shattered pieces of a broken mirror. Both children had tried to attack her too, so she had to defend herself. She claimed she was the innocent one and that Carla had attempted to murder not only her husband but her as well.

Remembering the abuse she herself had experienced growing up, Marie suspected there was more to story than the wife was admitting. Walking over to Carla, who was slowly regaining consciousness, Marie put her hand gently on the girl's arm. When she moved the sheet away and opened the girl's gown, her suspicions were confirmed. Fresh bruises from recent beatings told the real story.

As Carla regained consciousness, her first words were about Lily. Was she hurt badly? Would she be OK? After reassuring her that Lily would be fine, Marie held Carla's hand until she fell asleep. The girl's situation reminded Marie of her own sad, loveless childhood and of the abuse she had endured at Drayton House. Ben had been a ray of hope for her then. Marie wondered if she might, in turn, be a ray of hope for Carla now.

The policeman and Marie managed to uncover the true story about what had happened to Carla and Lily. Lily, now fully awake, corroborated Carla's story; and officers who were called to the scene said that they had gotten a call from concerned neighbors, who had heard the girls screaming. After Mrs. Andrews told them about the previous abuse charges that had been brought against Bernard, the officer called in detectives, who took the case from there.

As soon as Carla got out of Recovery, she was moved to Lily's room so that the two could keep each other company. This also made it easier for visitors to see both girls at once. Ben and Jan visited them every day, as did Marie. The big surprise was the way Nicholas bonded with both girls. He was totally enamored with sweet, delicate Lily and delighted in delivering dolls and stuffed animals to her room. But he was also strangely drawn to the sad, withdrawn Carla and made every effort to engage her in games or make her laugh.

Looking at Carla reminded Nicholas of his own childhood agonies. Offering her kindness and understanding not only helped Carla begin to trust and love but also furthered Nicholas' own healing.

On the day the girls were to be released from the hospital, Marie, Nicholas, Jan, and Ben met at the diner for breakfast. Ben mentioned that he and Jan had been planning to have Lily on overnight visits once they were married but now Carla had also found a place in their hearts. Each girl needed love and a good home, and he wished that someone could adopt both of them. However, he didn't hold much hope that would happen, especially since Lily was labeled "unadoptable."

Giving Marie a quick wink, Nicholas admitted that he and Marie felt the same way about the girls and hoped they might be able to do something about it. His plan was to have his legal team get Lily's "unadoptable" status overturned and then he and Marie could adopt both girls.

"Ben, you've been like a father to Marie over the years, standing up for her when she needed protection, demonstrating how bright she was when others thought she was retarded, and later helping her to get through medical school. If we succeed in adopting these girls, you and Jan are going to be their grandparents. You can dote on them and have as many sleepovers with them as you want."

"And all of us 'unadoptables' will now be a family," Marie added softly.

# ABOUT THE AUTHOR

PJ Dischino began writing at the age of eighty by creating and publishing a novel geared toward teens. Now eighty four, she has written her first adult romantic novel. The author refers to herself as a "Grandma Moses" of writing. She feels no one is ever too old to accomplish a new challenge.

www.ingramcontent.com/pod-product-compliance
Lightning Source LLC
Chambersburg PA
CBHW070840120626
46556CB00002B/816